KT-563-127

# A SHADOWED FATE

# A SHADOWED FATE

## Marty Ambrose

This first world edition published 2019
in Great Britain and 2020 in the USA by
SEVERN HOUSE PUBLISHERS LTD of
Eardley House, 4 Uxbridge Street, London W8 7SY.
Trade paperback edition first published
in Great Britain and the USA 2020 by
SEVERN HOUSE PUBLISHERS LTD.

Copyright © 2019 by Marty Ambrose.

All rights reserved including the right of
reproduction in whole or in part in any form.
The right of Marty Ambrose to be
identified as the author of this work has been
asserted in accordance with the Copyright,
Designs & Patents Act 1988.

British Library Cataloguing in Publication Data
*A CIP catalogue record for this title is available from the British Library.*

ISBN-13: 978-0-7278-8992-8 (cased)
ISBN-13: 978-1-78029-662-3 (trade paper)
ISBN-13: 978-1-4483-0361-8 (e-book)

This is a work of fiction. Names, characters, places and incidents
are either the product of the author's imagination or are used fictitiously.
Except where actual historical events and characters are being described
for the storyline of this novel, all situations in this publication are
fictitious and any resemblance to actual persons, living or dead,
business establishments, events or locales is purely coincidental.

*All Severn House titles are printed on acid-free paper.*

Severn House Publishers support the Forest Stewardship Council™ [FSC™],
the leading international forest certification organisation.
All our titles that are printed on FSC certified paper carry the FSC logo.

MIX
Paper from
responsible sources
FSC® C013056

Typeset by Palimpsest Book Production Ltd.,
Falkirk, Stirlingshire, Scotland.
Printed and bound in Great Britain by
TJ International, Padstow, Cornwall.

*For Jim – my dear hubby*

# ACKNOWLEDGMENTS

I always have so many people to thank for helping me realize my dream of creating historical fiction that I hardly know where to begin. But I have to start with my husband, Jim, who learned Italian, drove me from coast to coast on the *Autostrada*, and translated when I was doing primary research on this book in Italy. *Grazie mille, amore mio.* Secondly, I have to give my endless gratitude to my mom and sister, E.A., who have always provided me with such loving encouragement on my writing/life journey.

Also, I'm so appreciative of the beautiful Italian people. As we traveled around the country, everyone was patient and generous, making Jim and me part of their lives as if we were family. In particular, many thanks to everyone at the *Terme* in Bagni di Lucca – especially Vergilio, the town historian who shared information about Byron and Shelley, which provided many insights for my research.

On the publishing side, I would not have been able to continue this trilogy without the support of my amazing agent, Nicole Resciniti, and the lovely people at Severn House: Kate Lyall-Grant and my editor, Sara Porter. You are all the best!

Lastly, it's been a labor of love to write about Claire Clairmont, the missing voice of the Byron/Shelley circle.

*Era già l'ora che volge il disio*
*ai navicanti e 'ntenerisce il core*
*lo dì c'han detto ai dolciamici addio;*

*e che lo novo peregrin d'amore*
*punge, se ode squilla di lontano*
*che paia il giorno pianger che si more;*

Now – in the hour that melts with homesick yearning
The hearts of seafarers who've had to say
Farewell to those they love, that very morning –

Hour when the new-made pilgrim on his way
Feels a sweet pang go through him, if he hears
Far chimes that seem to knell the dying day

Dante, Canto of the Purgatory
*Purgatorio:* Canto VIII

# ONE

'My Paradise had still been incomplete.'

*The Prophecy of Dante*, I, 27

*Florence, Italy*
*July 1873*

It hardly seems possible that one's entire existence can be completely upended in the blink of an eye, but it happened to me, so I know it to be true.

During one balmy Florentine evening, in a moment hovering between past and present, I experienced a shift that made me see my life anew – a vision of the future that dawned with bright and previously unimagined chances. I cannot say for certain where all this newfound optimism would end, but my world *had* changed, and I now looked toward the coming days as full of possibilities that I could scarcely have even dreamed about a week ago.

I, Claire Clairmont, dared not do so.

Living in genteel poverty in Florence with my niece, Paula, and her daughter, our lives had become a constant cycle of budgeting our *lire* and scheming for new ways to keep our shabby rented rooms at the Palazzo Cruciato from falling into complete disrepair. It took all the wily craftiness that I had learned over a long life to maintain some semblance of respectability in this ancient Italian city, but I was nothing if not resourceful.

In my youth, I had traveled the world by my wits alone – seen Mount Vesuvius at dawn, survived a frigid winter in Czarist Moscow, flirted with Frenchmen in my cottage at Montmartre. Always looking for another adventure. Always seeking another way to survive. But having entered my eighth decade, in truth the penury had begun to wear thin. My daily existence seemed to stretch on without any promise of a new dawn, causing me to make my will, pay for my funeral, and anticipate the time when I would see my beloved deceased daughter, Allegra, in heaven. The next world seemed to beckon with whispers about the Great Beyond – the sweet hope of my adopted Catholic religion.

But that had all changed when I learned that she might still be alive.

Allegra.

*Allegrina* – as she was called by her Italian nursemaid so long ago – and the light of my life.

My daughter by one of the most famous (and infamous) literati of his era: George Gordon, Lord Byron, the Romantic poet whose reputation had soared ever higher during the fifty-or-so years since his death fighting for Greek independence at Missolonghi.

Brilliant, charming, outrageous, and cruel.

Byron could be all of those things – and more. I had mourned his death – as I did for my stepsister, Mary Shelley, almost three decades later when she departed this world, feted and famous, from her home in England, surrounded by a loving family. She and I had outlived the men who enchanted and betrayed us.

Byron – my lover. Percy Bysshe Shelley – her lover and husband.

Their names now caused awed silence to descend, but I knew them when they were young and passionate and careless. Profoundly talented, of course. But when Byron headed off to the doomed mission in Greece, and Shelley foolhardily took his sailboat into the Bay of Lerici near La Spezia during a violent storm, they never had a thought about those left behind.

Byron. Shelley. Mary.

All of them gone.

Yet I lived on.

I was the last member of our magic circle from that 'haunted summer' of 1816 in Geneva, when we would gather each night as the thunderstorms rolled in, and the lightning danced around us with a wild ferocity. We told ghost stories huddled around the firelight at Byron's Villa Diodati in the evenings – frightening ourselves with deliberate intent. For that brief time, we shared an interlude that defined the rest of our lives: Shelley and Byron created poetry of unparalleled beauty; Mary first penned *Frankenstein*; Byron's erratic physician, Polidori, wrote *The Vampyre*, and I conceived my daughter with Byron.

We lived with a heated intensity that I'd never experienced again until a few days ago when I was held at gunpoint by a killer, and my old friend Edward Trelawny had arrived unexpectedly in Florence as part of my rescue. Afterwards, he revealed the bare details about the truth of my daughter's fate – she had survived the typhus epidemic that swept through her convent school. He had kept that secret from me for many years even as he professed to care deeply for me. His treachery cut deep. It had taken me days to summon the strength to see him afterwards.

Eventually, I relented, and he arrived at the Palazzo Cruciato during teatime with a bouquet of white roses and a shamed expression.

'Claire, thank you for agreeing to see me. I promised to tell you everything that I knew about Allegra, and I am here to do just that. I have no excuse for my behavior, but I ask you to listen and not condemn me,' Trelawny entreated me as he strolled across my sitting room – still a handsome, imposing figure with broad shoulders and silver-streaked hair that flowed to his shoulders. But his bearded face bore the weathered traces of his age and days at sea with its rough, reddened skin and feathering of lines that radiated from his piercing eyes. He also had a slight stoop from a musket ball being lodged in his upper back, courtesy of an assassination attempt during the Greek War of Independence.

An aging corsair, still lethal in his own way – and ever conscious of the swath he cut through the society of women with tales of his wartime adventures.

Such an intriguing mixture of courage and vanity.

Irresistible in his own way.

Except that he had added 'deceiver' to his repertoire of qualities, something not easily accepted.

From my wingback chair near the open window that over-
looked the Boboli Gardens, I scanned the features of this man
at once familiar and distant to me. I, too, had fallen under his
spell long ago. *Trelawny*. I once believed him to be my friend
and supporter – and I had not seen him in several decades,
though we had always corresponded. I first met him in Pisa
in 1822 when he had presented himself to the Shelleys and
me as a retired naval lieutenant (not exactly true) who could
teach Shelley the complexities of handling a sailing boat
(mostly true). A self-styled Byronic hero who edged around
honesty as if it were a thorny wood, but I had always liked
him. That made his deception even more heart-wrenching.

'You have hurt me with your lies,' I began, trying hard to
keep my voice calm and even.

'I know.' Just that – nothing more. What else could be said?

'It has been so long since we have met – and much has just
happened – but I will withhold judgment about your deception
until I hear what you have to share.' I gestured for him to take
the matching chair across the tea table from me. 'I must warn
you that things have changed in the last few years; my circumstances have been greatly reduced after my disastrous farming
investment in Austria. I am wary of those whom I cannot fully
. . . trust.' It had been a poor financial choice to help my
nephew, a risk that had depleted the last of my Shelley bequest.
But my family could always make me abandon common sense.

'When did a lack of money ever matter to us?' He slid on
to the well-worn velvet cushion, stretching out his long legs
encased in breeches and riding boots. 'Possessing the richness
of spirit and soul greatly outweighs actual wealth.'

'So true, but bills cannot be paid with good intentions.' I
lifted a brow in irony as I shifted my glance toward the kitchen
where Paula was occupied in making afternoon tea. 'I have
the welfare of my niece and her daughter, Georgiana, to
consider now . . . and the world is not always kind to those
who have entered their autumnal years.' I knew only too well
from my mirror's reflection that my Mediterranean charms
had faded somewhat – my olive skin bore a few wrinkles and
my dark curls had threads of gray, though I fancied the sparkle
in my eyes remained undimmed.

But I was no longer a young woman.

'You will always be that spirited beauty I met in Pisa – so full of life, so vivacious – with the voice of an angel.'

I smiled, smoothing down the folds of my yellow cotton dress with its tiny, carefully mended holes in the fabric. All of my dresses had seen better days, to say the least. 'The lessons of life have changed me, as you might expect. A woman of my station is relegated to her place – no matter what – and living in Florence has taught me the added lesson that money is both the great blessing and bane of our later existence. I cannot afford to make . . . mistakes.' My glance met his squarely. 'You and I played with life and put ourselves – and others – in jeopardy at one time, but no more. People connected with the secrets about Allegra's fate have already died, and we must not allow any further bloodshed.'

Of course, I meant Father Gianni, my priest and confidant who had been stabbed at the Basilica di San Lorenzo only about a fortnight ago. He had been assisting me in my search for the truth behind Allegra's fate, researching old records from the convent at Bagnacavallo where she had supposedly died when she was still a child. It turned out that his killer was our landlord, Matteo Ricci – a thief and rogue – who wanted to profit from the valuable Byron/Shelley memorabilia that I had shared with Father Gianni on my quest. After his arrest, Matteo had confessed that his gambling debts had driven him to such an evil act when Father Gianni tried to stop him from stealing my correspondence. Truly, I would never have involved my priest if I had known about Matteo's desperation, but it could not be undone.

I would always feel regret for my actions.

And sadness.

'From what the police told me when I stopped by the *commissariato di pubblica sicurezza* this morning, Matteo will pay – murder is punishable by death. And by God, he deserves to be hanged for such a heinous act.' Trelawny's face hardened into deep, harsh crevices. 'He will be damned in the next world – if one believes in that kind of thing.'

He did not, as I knew only too well.

My hand covered the small gold locket hanging from a fine

chain at my neck – my mother's last gift to me, given to her by my father, whom I never knew. I treasured it, even though my mother never approved of me – or my life. 'Perhaps Matteo deserves no mercy from us, but divine forgiveness may still await him.'

'Not likely.'

In truth, I could not disagree. 'Sadly, Father Gianni was not able to receive word from Bagnacavallo, so all I know is that Allegra did not die at the convent and, for some reason, you and Byron hid that fact from me – along with a valuable piece of artwork that could have greatly relieved my poverty.' Almost choking on the words, I pointed at the pen-and-ink sketch on textured paper that lay on the tea table. It depicted the Egyptian obelisk that stood in the nearby Boboli Gardens, drawn by the famous Italian artist, Giuseppe Cades – given to me only recently when it was discovered by Polidori's nephew. A Florentine landmark, the needle-shaped granite monument had been erected in ancient Egypt and brought to Italy, eventually finding a home behind the nearby Pitti Palace. It held special meaning for me because Byron and I met there for the last time in 1822 – and secretly buried a memento of our daughter at its base. 'I would like to know why you both lied.'

His face shuttered with shades of contrition. 'May I first say how sorry I am? I never meant to cause you harm.'

I did not reply.

'My only defense is that Byron swore me to secrecy.' He took in a deep breath and picked up the sketch, tracing carefully the edges of the drawing. 'When he gave this to me, it was with the promise that I never reveal it, or Allegra's true fate, to you – and I followed his request.'

'More's the pity that you agreed to such falsehoods,' I said sharply, feeling a mixture of anger and bitterness. 'It is the worst type of betrayal – separating me from my own daughter when I was basically alone in the world and would have cherished every moment with her. To be honest, if I did not want to know the whole story that you came to tell me, I would never want to see you again – *ever.*'

Wincing, he glanced down briefly. 'You have every right to

be angry with me, but Byron made his case so strongly that I dared not go against his wishes. It seemed the best way at the time to protect both you and Allegra . . .'

Moments passed in silence as I contemplated all of the time that I had missed with my daughter. Moments that a mother cherished – the smiles and the tears. When I bade farewell to Allegra, she had been only two, and my memories had grown hazy, though not forgotten. Time had blurred some of the past.

I never wanted to give her up, but as a woman of twenty who was alone without resources, it made sense for her to live with Byron; he had wealth and social standing in Italy, not to mention fame. I did not anticipate that he would not allow me to see her when he lived in Ravenna, and I in Pisa.

I had hated him for that.

'Do you still think about him?' Trelawny's voice threaded through the quietness. He did not need to say his name: I knew.

'When do I ever *not* think of him?' Sighing, I gazed out over the Boboli Gardens' gently unfolding terraces, flowering trees, and Roman statues. Its lush beauty had been my consolation for many years . . . and the scene of my greatest pain.

'There has never been anyone like him before or since – brilliant and brave, yet stubborn and foolhardy. When he said he hardly knew himself to be more than a chameleon, it was true. He was my friend and later my comrade-in-arms but, at times, something about his nature remained elusive.' Trelawny spoke slowly, as if he was working out pieces to a puzzle. 'Byron was always the shadow between us, was he not, Claire? How could I ever compete with a ghost?'

Turning from the window, I regarded him with a thoughtful gaze. 'Perhaps the ghost was not him, but Allegra.'

'Or both.'

'Possibly . . . I think he was somewhat jealous of you,' I added in a slightly lighter tone. 'How often is it that a poet sees the living embodiment of his own poetic creations? When you suddenly appeared in Pisa after fighting in the Napoleonic Wars, seemingly more of a Byronic hero than Byron himself, he must have been quite chagrined. Or so I have heard.'

'He was courageous, Claire,' he said with quiet emphasis. 'Never doubt it.'

'If you say so.' I shrugged. Still smarting over this conspiracy that Byron had engineered, I was in no mood to hear anything favorable about him. 'But here we are, speaking of *him* again when we should be focused on what happened to Allegra—'

Just then, Paula entered, carrying the tea tray, complete with my beloved antique china teapot, three cups and saucers, and a little tin that housed my favorite oolong tea. I never lost my taste for its deep and bitter flavor. 'You two seem rather engrossed in your conversation,' she observed in a cool voice.

Trelawny immediately rose and took the tray from her, setting it on the small table in front of me and carefully placing the sketch to the side.

'*Grazie.*' She slid on to the settee opposite our chairs and began the ritual of measuring out the black tea, her delicate, cameo-like features bent over her task. Scooping out one spoon at a time into the teapot, she then poured in the hot water with efficient motions born of long practice. 'I hope that I did not miss anything important.'

Trelawny shook his head. 'I was just about to tell your aunt everything I knew about Allegra.'

'Indeed?' She kept her focus on the tea ritual, brushing back a stray blond hair. 'I, for one, would like to hear *why* you lied to Aunt Claire for so long – she has been distressed for days over your actions. It does not seem like the behavior of someone who cares about her, knowing how much she grieved her daughter's supposed death. Certainly, we intend to hear you out, but do not expect approval—'

'Or forgiveness,' I added.

'Once you hear the entire story, I am hoping that you will understand why I remained silent for so long.' He seated himself again, watching Paula with a slight smile. 'You are very much like your aunt – spirited and independent.'

'We have both had to fend for ourselves.' Paula strained the dark liquid into one of the cups. 'Milk and sugar?'

'Neither – thank you.'

She handed it to him.

As Trelawny made more small talk while Paula poured the other two cups, I watched him try to work his magic on my niece. At once both deferential and masculine, he was an unusual blend of gentleman and outlaw. It was an attractive combination, but what truly drew me to him was the kindness that I discovered lay behind his swagger. Never a man to trifle with, Trelawny always protected those he cared about. Except this time . . .

Paula and I sipped our tea, waiting for him to begin. Time seemed to pause in that hushed room in spite of the ormolu clock on the fireplace mantle ticking with a steady rhythm, the pendulum swinging back and forth with a staccato clicking sound – each tap signaling a chance for Trelawny to render his tale.

Eventually, he leaned forward, his elbows resting on his thighs. 'As you know, when Byron left Genoa for Greece in the autumn of 1823 to join in the War of Independence against the Turks, he asked me to join him. Of course, I could not turn him down. What man would not welcome the chance for honor and glory, especially for the Greek cause? I set sail the same day that I received his note and joined him in Cephalonia. Pietro Gamba had already made the crossing from Italy—'

'Ah, yes. Pietro – the brother of Byron's last mistress, Teresa,' I could not resist interjecting, a slight edge in my tone.

'He was a fine young man – loyal and strong-minded. He fought on in Greece after Byron's demise but, sadly, also died quite young.' A brief melancholy shadow crossed Trelawny's face. Then he continued, 'But I digress . . . When I arrived in Cephalonia, the situation was dire. Military factions fighting each other, no clear battle plans, and little money to finance an army. Byron's presence was most welcome since he showed surprising diplomatic skill at bringing the men together – and he also brought a huge war chest of gold to finance the first campaign.'

'Byron? A diplomat?' Paula said, her brow furrowed with puzzlement as she swung her glance in my direction. 'But that is nothing like the man you have told me about, Aunt Claire. The poetic genius who treated people so carelessly and roamed around Europe without clear purpose. How could *he* have been such a hero?'

'I suppose my view of him has been somewhat colored by

his treatment of our daughter – perhaps unfairly when that image is placed next to the man he might have become in Greece,' I admitted reluctantly. But I was not ready to forgive Byron – even if he had found a late-life redemption.

'Perhaps somewhat,' Paula murmured.

If there was a tinge of reproach in her words, I did not hear it, though my heart beat a little faster, anticipating what Trelawny was about to say.

'I would have laid down my life for Byron – we all would have because we fought for a just cause and we trusted him.' He stared off into the distance at some memory that I could not share . . . a lost horizon of a soldier's world where men took on hardships that tested their mettle and power. 'Byron and I drilled the troops in the morning and found ourselves dining alone in the evenings. Pietro would fall asleep, but Byron seemed oddly energized by the constant sense of danger. He thrived on it. He was not writing then, but his conversations flowed richly about politics, his life in England, his loves—'

'You wrote about much of that in your memoir,' I cut in with some impatience. Trelawny had published his *Recollections of the Last Days of Shelley and Byron* about fifteen years earlier; it gave some military details of the Greek conflict, but little of the emotional details that I wanted to hear – or the facts about my daughter. I had but skimmed it, feeling that Trelawny had exaggerated their exploits, but perhaps he had not done so.

'Yes, but of course I omitted Byron's comments about you, Claire, and the guilt he felt about Allegra. He mentioned it night after night. I heard the stories of how you met in England and found each other again in Geneva with Mary and Shelley at the Villa Diodati, sailed the lake in between the storms, gathered in the evenings to philosophize on life . . . and, later, how he learned that you were going to bear his child.'

I sighed. 'It was a . . . remarkable time. We were so young and so full of optimism that it seems difficult even to remember who I was then, except that I never wanted the summer to end.'

'Nor did he – apparently,' Trelawny added with a half-smile. 'Unfortunately, life never stands still, does it?'

I shook my head.

He drained his teacup in one long, deep swallow. 'Events in Cephalonia moved rather quickly once we began training the Souliotes for the first big offensive against the Turks; at first, we had only minor skirmishes but made plans eventually to attack the fortress at Lepanto. I believe it was in February that Byron traveled to Missolonghi to bring the military factions together, while he sent me to the north for meetings with envoys from the London Greek Committee. All went well for me, but not so for him. Missolonghi was a depressing place – a town built on a marsh, full of mosquitoes and malaria, where the sea and sky seemed to blend into one surreal, cloudy landscape. Sieges had become commonplace and none of the commanders could agree how to attack the Turks.' His voice shook slightly. 'Frustrated with the constant squabbles around him, Byron rode out from the town on horseback and was caught in a rainstorm. Not long afterwards, he grew feverish, then weakened quickly, with only his servant Fletcher to attend to him at first . . .'

As Trelawny's voice trailed off, I found myself unable to speak. Certainly, I had read his account of Byron's death in Greece in Trelawny's *Recollections*, but absorbing the details of my lost lover's final days ignited a new spark of compassion within me. Taking on the role of a warrior-leader, Byron had isolated himself. And he had been so long out of England that he lost contact – except through occasional letters – with those who were, at one time, so much a part of his life. I knew the latter part only too well. Much as I loved my adopted country, there is a loneliness in being in a foreign land that never really goes away. A bittersweet longing for one's native soil. I could imagine his staring out over the Adriatic Sea, thinking of his dear Newstead Abbey and wondering if all of his English friends had forgotten him.

I cleared my throat. 'He must have known that he would not survive Greece.'

Trelawny nodded with a grim twist to his mouth.

'It sounds as if that was the way he wanted to die.' Paula solemnly refilled Trelawny's cup. 'Perhaps it redeemed him – if only in his own mind.'

Reaching out, I touched my niece's cheek. 'Your kind nature shames me, my dear. I have been pitiless in my own behavior and held malice in my heart toward Byron. But now, when I hear about his valor, I must admit that he became a different man to the one whom I recall.' I smiled at her blink of surprise. 'Don't look so shocked. I have been reflecting for the last couple of days and realized that my lingering rancor against him will not change what happened.'

'You may even find forgiveness . . . for *both* of us when you hear the rest of my narrative,' Trelawny added as he held up the obelisk sketch. 'Before Byron left for Missolonghi, he showed this drawing to me and said he kept it with him at all times. Then he told me what was hidden at the obelisk's base in the Boboli Gardens: a box with Allegra's lock of hair that you placed there together.'

*The enamel box.*

We buried it there.

Now it was Paula's turn to offer me a touch of reassurance, since she had learned about it only recently. 'It must have been difficult for you to keep that secret for so long, but I understand why you kept it hidden. It held such a personal sentiment for you.'

'No one knew about it – or at least I thought that to be the case.' I bit my lip to keep it from trembling. 'Byron had come to Florence with the box, six months after Allegra supposedly died, and we placed it there so something of her would survive. I suppose I wanted to keep those precious moments to myself because it was a private moment and the last time I ever saw Byron.' Sighing, I remembered his parting words of love and guilt; he had looked weary beyond his years – a man who had experienced too much in life. 'I had no idea until I dug it up at the Boboli Gardens a few nights ago that he had left a message in the box saying our daughter had not died, but had been hidden for her own safety.'

With dawning realization, Paula said slowly, 'He never meant for you to read it, did he?'

'No.' I could still feel his cold cheek against mine when he kissed me farewell and extracted a promise that I would never look at the contents of the box again.

'I am so sorry, Aunt.'

Leveling a glare at Trelawny, I continued, 'But *you* knew.' It was not a question.

'Byron told me in our last conversation – along with his confession that Allegra survived her days in the convent school—'

'Why did you deceive me?' I demanded as a surge of ire rose up inside of me. 'I trusted you after those early years in Pisa when you said how much I meant to you – and, later, when I returned from Russia and you asked me to marry you. If I had agreed to become your wife, would you have hidden the secret from me even then?'

I heard Paula take in a quick breath.

'Yes,' he replied.

I slammed my cup in the saucer and it broke apart, the fragile china cracking into several jagged sections that fell to the carpet. Instantly, Trelawny knelt, scooped up the fragments, and set them on the tea table. He then took my hands and checked them over, tracing my palm with a light touch. 'No cuts – thank goodness.'

'It is hardly your concern.' Pulling back, I searched his face for the honest and true man that I had once known. 'It seems as if I was gravely mistaken to place my faith in you, Edward.'

'Please . . . I am not finished.' Trelawny stiffened at my indictment of his deception. 'You must know all of it now, though you may not want to hear it. Byron had me swear an oath not to tell you about Allegra because he said that it would have endangered both of your lives. When he lived in Ravenna, talk of revolution was in the air and someone tried to shoot him when he went riding in the pine forests near Filetto – the gunman missed. Afterwards, Byron became concerned – not for himself but for Allegra. He placed her in the Convent of Bagnacavello for her protection but, only months later, an assassin tried to kill *her.* She escaped death only because the Abbess caught the intruder by surprise: he had appeared in Allegra's room with a knife while she lay sleeping. The nun shouted for help, but he escaped; he seemed to fit the description of a man who worked in the household of Ludovico di Breme. Afterwards, Byron knew it was no longer safe for your daughter to remain there.'

'Di Breme? The man who came to visit Byron when we were in Geneva? You told me only recently in the Boboli Gardens that Byron was alarmed by his appearance – especially after my suspicious fall at Castle Chillon.' I simply stared at him, trying to make sense of his story. It was as if I could grasp only echoes of this bizarre retelling of the past – nothing seemed to fit together, now or then. 'But why?'

'Byron came to know di Breme later in Italy – as a poet and revolutionary – but he chose not to share that part of the story with me, except that di Breme had a servant named Stefano who he thought had tried to harm Allegra. So when the typhus epidemic swept through the convent a few months later, he faked Allegra's death and sent her into hiding.' Trelawny paused, letting the weight of his words sink in.

'Can it be true?' Paula said, her hand shaking as she set the teacup down. 'Why would anyone want to kill a child?'

My breathing grew labored as I struggled with my emotions. I had longed to know the whole truth behind my daughter's supposed death, but this revelation was hardly what I had expected. A potential killer at the convent? It was almost too terrible to believe, but Trelawny's clear and direct gaze told me everything I needed to know about the veracity of his story. It explained much about his part in Byron's subterfuge, and the reason for the two of them to have created such a scheme.

'It was chaotic in Italy at the time – the country was on the brink of war against its Austrian oppressors – and Byron was caught up in the midst of it in Ravenna because of his asso-ciation with Teresa and her family,' Trelawny explained to Paula as he struggled to his feet, a bit more slowly than I remembered from the last time I saw him. 'They were heavily involved in a secret and ancient society . . .'

A realization began to stir inside of me. 'The Carbonari?'

'You knew?' He touched my shoulder gently.

'Only recently.' I recounted how Father Gianni had noticed a Carbonari charcoal burner symbol drawn on the page of one of Byron's letters, and told me what it meant. 'He is the one who explained that they were a secret society, built around the trade of charcoal, and that Byron had likely become a member.'

'So the priest guessed about the Carbonari connection to Byron.' Trelawny frowned as he rubbed the back of his neck in an absent gesture. 'It may be a coincidence that he discovered it at the same time that Matteo confronted him at the basilica, but it does seem to add another element to Father Gianni's death.'

'Indeed.' My anger had dissipated somewhat, but I had even more concerns about what had happened. Was Father Gianni's death more than a simple murder and, if so, how did it link to Byron's role with the Carbonari?

Perhaps nothing was as it seemed . . . and never would be again.

'Can you see why I never dared to write about this part of my days with Byron or tell you about Allegra?' he pressed me with a note of urgency in his voice. 'I gave him my word and believed that, in doing so, it would save Allegra from another potential threat to her life. Many people wanted Byron dead, both in Italy and, later, Greece; he had made many enemies, and they would have done anything to kill him or anyone related to him.'

Stubbornly, I averted my head. 'He could have sent Allegra to live with me in Pisa, where I was staying with Mary and Shelley; we were far from Ravenna.'

'Surely you realize that option would have been rife with danger. Shelley was known as an atheist with revolutionary ideas; he was watched by the police. Bringing your daughter into that situation would have made her safety – and yours – even more fraught with peril.'

'What about later, after Byron had died?' I pressed him as I swung my glance back in his direction. 'Why did you not tell me then?'

'I did not know if the danger was over,' he said simply. 'Nor do I even now.'

In my heart I knew he was right, but I could not say it. Not yet.

Paula pressed her hands to her cheeks, grown even paler. 'This whole story is all so utterly unbelievable, with talk of secret societies and assassins – and even more so because of the events of the last two or so weeks. Murderous landlords.

Secrets and lies. I feel that our tranquil life in Florence is gone forever—'

'I wish that we did not have to burden you with the knowledge of the dark time that occurred long before you were born,' I began, 'but we have little choice now, since things have been set into motion.'

'I know.' Her tone conveyed disapproval as she rose and lifted the tea tray once more. 'I need to put Georgiana down for her nap, but I urge you to proceed cautiously, if we are to find your long-lost daughter. We cannot allow Georgiana to be placed at risk.' She exited the room with a graceful dignity – and a resolve that brooked no disagreement.

Her words left a wide swath of remorse around me, a wave that reflected on the headstrong impulsivity of my youth. Certainly, I had always set my own sails and headed out into seas that had no clear destination; I never cared . . . until I had my own daughter. Then I tried to steer a more conventional course for a while but, once she departed this world, I had little reason to embrace the commonplace life. I never wanted it.

Trelawny touched my shoulder. 'Paula will come to understand.'

'What exactly?'

'That we came to maturity during a different age – and were bound by the desire for freedom.' He moved toward the large window and gazed outward as he echoed my thoughts. 'We rejected a tame and tedious journey through life, wanting to experience every moment as if it were our last. Remember what Byron said: "The great object of life is sensation – to feel we exist, even if it be in pain." No truer words were spoken.' He turned back to me. 'Do not regret that, Claire. Many women never have even a day when they are not thinking their own thoughts or striving for their own goals. You have lived on your own terms – always – and must always do so.'

'Even at seventy-five?' I could not resist adding.

'*Especially* at this age. Peace and quiet is for those in the grave – not us.' A smile touched the corners of his mouth. 'We must vow to push against the darkness with all of our might.'

In spite of my emotional turmoil, a tiny glow of excitement lit inside me and I smiled back at him.

'I see the Claire that I once knew in your eyes again – that spark of vibrance,' he said, drawing near again. 'I have missed it.'

'There has been little of that joy in our lives recently,' I admitted.

He picked up the obelisk drawing again and studied it. 'I wish Byron had told me more about Allegra's fate, but he did not give me further details. If he had, and I had learned where she was hidden, I would have found a way to make certain that she wanted for nothing over the years . . . I did everything I could to reach him in Missolonghi when I heard he was so ill, crossing over the mountains to be by his side, walking the last ten miles on foot in the mud, but he was already dead by the time I arrived.'

'It caught the world unawares.' Even after the stretch of time, my breath caught in my throat at the word, and I remembered how the news had stunned everyone. Dazed, the great poet Tennyson carved the words *Byron is dead* on a stone, sensing that with his demise, a cold wind now blew across the world.

News of his passing had reached me during the summer of 1824 in Russia, where I was living with the Zotoff family as governess to their daughter, Betsy. We had traveled to their summer home outside Moscow – a low, wooden manor house that stood in the middle of five hundred acres – and I was walking near the river at sunset, watching the violet clouds edged in gold, when Countess Zotoff approached me with a newspaper in hand. Knowing nothing of my relationship with him, she related in stilted French that my countryman had died in Greece. A hero's death, she said – then followed with a whispered prayer.

Mutely, I managed a nod.

And the moment passed as if it had never occurred.

Weeks later, when I heard the great bell of the Zagorski Monastery ring early on a Sunday morning, I burst into tears for what might have been.

'Claire?' Trelawny's voice brought me back to the present.

Slowly, my focus came back to my sitting room. So ordinary and familiar, yet somehow different. Touching my locket again, I took a moment to trace the delicate filigree as something solid and real. 'You know that I never cared to dwell too long in the past, so I find it somewhat difficult to go back there. I appreciate your telling me everything, but it has . . . many shadows.'

'I am your friend once more?'

Still holding the pendant, I heard Father Gianni's admonition deep in my heart. *You must forgive those who wronged you. Compassione. You must have compassion.* I had forgiven my mother for disowning me, but that was another matter . . .

'We shall see.' It was the best that I could offer him.

'I understand.' He touched my arm. 'Perhaps as you consider what I have told you, in time you will even come to forgive me.'

It was all too new, too raw, for me to even consider that possibility.

'This may help to change your mind.' Trelawny reached into his coat pocket and produced a small leather portfolio bound by a single strap. 'When Byron came to Ravenna in 1820 and found himself in the middle of an uprising, he decided to keep his own account of the Carbonari – and his role in their secret society. It covers everything from his arrival in Ravenna to the end of the revolt fourteen months later.' He paused, turning the journal over in his hand to reveal the etched symbol of a charcoal burner on the back. 'Byron gave it to his Venetian friend, Angelo Mengaldo, a good man, but he feared if the memoir became public, it would endanger many lives. So Mengaldo burned it – sight unseen. Fortunately, the Cades drawing remained with Byron's papers and ended up sent to Polidori, as you know.'

Ah, yes. John Polidori. Byron's physician in Geneva. So volatile. So eager to be a writer. So jealous of anyone in Byron's orbit. I had long thought Polidori was my enemy during the summer of 1816, but I had come to see that others may have been plotting against me.

I blinked in confusion. 'But if *Signor* Mengaldo destroyed the memoir, how do you come to have it?'

'Byron made a copy and entrusted it to me when we were in Greece, with the promise that I was to keep it hidden—'

I gave an exclamation of impatience. 'More lies and secrets?'

He shook his head. 'This document is much beyond that. It is the only known record of the Carbonari's innermost circles – not only Byron's activities, but locals who planned assassinations. Many of their actions would have been seen as treason, punishable by hanging, which is why I omitted these from my *Recollections.*'

'Does he mention di Breme's servant, Stefano?'

'Yes, but they were suspicions only – he never had proof.'

'He would be dead now in any case.' Still, it made me uneasy to have that question of his intent unanswered. 'I want to know about Allegra, but how would Byron's recollections be considered important today after the Risorgimento? That time is over, the revolution was eventually successful, and Italy is now unified. The Carbonari no longer exist.'

'Can you be so sure?'

A warning voice whispered in my head as I stared at the memoir.

I could not turn back now. Taking it from him, I noted cracks in the leather cover, deep-grooved and worn smooth over the years. 'I never quite perceived how hope and fear can merge into a new path at even this stage of life – this is a road that I cannot avoid.'

He leaned forward and whispered, 'Your courage would shame the most hardened soldier—'

A deliberate cough interrupted Trelawny, and I swiftly turned my head to see William Michael Rossetti standing in the doorway – the British tourist and Polidori's nephew who had come to Florence a little over two weeks ago to buy my letters for his new Shelley biography. Needless to say, it had not worked out quite the way he planned, but he had risked his life to save mine at the Boboli Gardens and I would always be grateful. Paula hovered behind him, holding hands with Raphael, our hired man and my niece's handsome lover.

'Mr Rossetti, how delightful to see you.' Instantly, I smiled in genuine delight at the sight of his pleasant features and gentlemanly air.

'Especially after our last meeting, which was extraordinary, to say the least,' he said with light irony as he shook hands first with Trelawny and then me. 'I thought it best to give you a little time to recover from the trauma, but I could not stay away any longer. Are you well enough to receive me?'

'Certainly.' I gestured for him to enter and take the chair next to me as I tucked the memoir out of sight. As he did so, Paula and Raphael seated themselves on the settee, completing our little group. Everyone whom I cared about was now present in this room, all familiar and dear, with the exception of Trelawny – he was, and would ever be, in disgrace. 'I did not have the chance to thank you for all of your efforts on my behalf, Mr Rossetti. You traveled all the way from England to Florence to buy my letters, but you ended up on a mission to right a long-standing wrong – truly, beyond kind.'

He bowed his head. 'It was my honor. As John Polidori's nephew, I could do no less to make up for his treatment of you.'

'You restored my faith in the future.' Needless to say, his connection to Polidori and additional revelations about his uncle's character had been a surprise when he revealed them. 'You brought word about Allegra and even restored this long-lost Cades sketch to my possession. I cannot express my gratitude to you.'

'I apologize that I could not tell you everything when I first arrived, but I was waiting for Trelawny to come.' He shook his head in regret. 'It might have prevented Father Gianni's murder – that is my one regret. He was a good man in every way.'

'You were not responsible for his death,' I assured him. 'Matteo had been plotting to steal my Byron/Shelley correspondence for many months.'

Raphael looked down and murmured something in Italian under his breath. A short, pungent curse. Paula clasped his hand and held it tightly. Their love seemed so palpable after the last few days; once hidden, it now had a living, breathing feeling that encircled them with shared happiness. Such a touching connection – 'such stuff as dreams are made on' as Shakespeare once said.

'Aunt Claire, you must tell us what you and Mr Trelawny discussed after I left,' Paula interjected in a firm tone. 'Is there any lingering danger after Matteo's arrest?'

I hesitated and motioned for Trelawny to respond.

He cleared his throat. 'I truly believe that Matteo committed the murder of Father Gianni for money and nothing more.'

Paula grimaced. 'And I had always thought our landlord was so kind. How mistaken we all were about him.'

'At least he is now in jail and cannot harm anyone else,' I added grimly. 'There are always those who hide behind the mask of pretense but, eventually, the illusion vanishes and the reality becomes clear. Even so, if Father Gianni had seen into Matteo's evil heart, he would have believed that he could turn the darkness to light – always the optimist about human nature.'

'So true.' Sighing, she leaned into Raphael's shoulder. His arm slid around her in a protective embrace.

'Still, perhaps if I had been more discreet about the true reason for my visit . . .' Mr Rossetti shrugged.

Trelawny shook his head. 'Matteo was hellbent on theft because of his gambling debts; you were not responsible for the priest's death.'

'I hope so.' Mr Rossetti's features brightened, though a trace of doubt lingered around his eyes. 'If I may ask, what do you intend to do with the newfound knowledge about your daughter's fate? I assume you will try to find her?'

'Indeed, yes,' I responded readily. 'Allegra would be in her late fifties now – perhaps with children and grandchildren of her own – and, hopefully, still living in Italy. Just imagine that my daughter might be residing scant kilometers from me. I almost dare not imagine it.'

Paula's lifted her head as she knit her brows in a frown. 'Do you think it's likely that she never even *suspected* her parentage? Just knowing how important family is to Italians, I cannot imagine that no one told her the truth or let something slip in her presence – especially after Byron died. Would you not agree, Raphael?'

'*Si*, but we Italians also know how to keep a secret,' he responded with a tightening of his protective embrace around her, but his words were meant for me. '*Mi scusi, per favore,* but if her guardians were told to hide her for her own safety, they would go to their graves with the truth.'

His meaning was clear – I had already entertained the possibility that the search for my daughter would prove to be a challenge and perhaps one that would not yield the outcome that I prayed for – I accepted that. But if it took the rest of my life, I would not stop until I knew for certain what had happened to Allegra.

'We must try, my friends. Faint heart never won success.' Trelawny rose from his chair, drawing himself up to his considerable height. Shoulders squared with confident poise, I knew he would be my ally in this quest to find out what happened to my daughter. Whether that made up for the past or not remained to be seen, but I would at least give him a chance to find redemption.

'I believe the expression is "faint heart never won fair maiden,"' I corrected him gently.

'Even better,' he agreed with a laugh.

'Shall you join us on our search, Mr Rossetti?' I asked, transferring my gaze to him with warm encouragement. 'Your company would certainly be most welcome.'

'Nothing would make me happier, Miss Clairmont, but I am afraid that I must return to England. I had a telegram just today from my sister, Christina, urging me to return home as soon as possible; my mother is ill.'

'Nothing serious, I trust?' I queried in concern.

Mr Rossetti shrugged. 'I cannot really say at this point. Mama is strong-willed but somewhat . . . advanced in years.'

He meant 'old.'

Why is it the young resort to these delicate euphemisms for a perfectly honest word? *Old.* I am old. I had lived for seven decades and, while there seemed little 'advancing' about the aging process, it was not without its own charms. I could speak my mind. I could make my own decisions. I could walk alone through the streets of Florence without a disapproving murmur from fellow English expatriates. In many ways, *molto bene.* If lonely moments drifted into my thoughts at the reality of outliving most of my dearest friends and relatives, well, what was the alternative? Life was meant for the living – not the dead.

'I shall say a novena to St Catherine of Siena for her,' I promised. 'Please do let me know how she fares.'

'When do you leave?' Paula asked.

'Tomorrow.'

'Then we must celebrate this evening – the five of us,' Trelawny pronounced. 'No sad faces or mournful thoughts. Let us dine out under the stars, drink wine from the Tuscan valley, and simply enjoy this time together. *La vita e bella*.'

'I know the perfect place, near the Ponte Vecchio,' Raphael enthused. '*Mio cugino*, Lorenzo, owns a restaurant on this side of the Arno – not fancy, just true Tuscan food that my cousin prepares himself.'

'Oh, yes.' Paula beamed at him, then turned to me. 'Aunt, can we go?'

I smiled. 'Who could turn down such an invitation?'

She rose quickly, pulling Raphael with her. 'I must go and wake Georgiana – then, if you will escort me to her friend's house, she can stay there while we have supper. Aunt Claire and I will wear white roses in our hair – for *Firenze*.'

She drew him out of room as she chattered away, and I heard their laughter follow them out of the room. 'Young love is such a sweet thing to behold.'

'Luckily, everyone in Italy is a cousin – *primo* or *secondo*, it's all family.'

Smiling, I stood up and shook out my long skirt, keeping the memoir hidden in its folds – I would share it with the rest of them later. Feeling some of my old buoyancy rising up inside once more, I vowed to embrace the joy of the moment, if only for this one night. Genteel poverty be damned. 'I, too, shall dress up for our evening out – my pink silk frock with lace trim. We will enjoy our supper and watch the sun set on the Arno as we toast to the future with chianti.'

'Thank you, my friend.' Trelawny clapped Mr Rossetti on the shoulder. 'Could anything be more needed? We survived the events of the last few days – alive and with hope – so we must make merry and let tomorrow bring what it may.'

'*Carpe diem* – yes, we must seize the day . . . or rather the night,' Mr Rossetti quipped. 'Beyond that, who knows?'

\* \* \*

And we were true to our vow.

We ate our supper sitting under the stars – feasted on *cinghiale*, wild boar served with antipasti. The wine flowed and I felt younger than I had in years. All the layers of heartache and poverty fell away. Our spirits soared. In the midst of it all, I watched Trelawny's face in the growing twilight. Even if he had held a terrible secret from me for so long, he had given me the gift of faith in this time and place. And not just this night of happiness, but a present that stretched out with a tantalizing offer of more than I could have hoped for: my daughter.

His eyes met mine and, in that moment, he knew that I would forgive him. Perhaps not today or tomorrow – but it would happen.

Raising his glass, he whispered, '*Amici.*'

*Friends.*

*Ah, but we had been something more . . . if only for a single night.*

After the moon rose, a cool breeze swept in from the Tuscan hillsides, bringing in a sweet fragrance of rose and lily; it mingled with an earthy whiff of ancient stone buildings and slight dampness from the Arno River. A perfect backdrop for the food of Florence with its golden olive oils, fresh herbs, and ripe, lush tomatoes. Raphael asked his cousin to serve *panforte* – a rich fruitcake – for dessert, and we celebrated his culinary skills and our good fortune at being able to partake of it.

Later, after a final course of coffee and biscotti around midnight, we made our way back to the Palazzo Cruciato through the narrow cobblestone streets now hushed in quiet darkness. All along the ancient palazzos, light streamed out of the occasional upper-story window, but most of the city had settled in for the night. As we ambled along, I dared to envision that light expanded even beyond these old and beautiful buildings, and the evening signaled a new beginning, an emergence into a future of good fortune. Perhaps the endless cycle of debt and defeat had finally passed.

When we arrived at our apartment, Trelawny ushered us inside and lit the gas lamp near the front door. As the flame illuminated our main parlor, I gasped and stepped backwards, clutching his arm. The room had been ransacked, with every piece of furniture tipped over, books strewn on the floor, and curtains ripped apart. Chaos and destruction everywhere.

'*Che disastro!*' Raphael held Paula back.

Grasping the lamp, Trelawny held it high and surveyed the wreckage. 'Stay here,' he whispered, gesturing for Raphael to follow him.

They disappeared inside as Paula clung to me, her hands trembling. I slipped my arm around her waist and held her close as we hovered in the doorway. 'We must be strong – all will be fine.' I knew better than to sound frightened; it would stoke her own fear even higher.

The minutes passed in silence, except for the sound of their footsteps on the stone floor.

Finally, Trelawny reappeared with the lamp, his features tight and grim. 'Come in – it is safe now.'

Relief flooded through me, though Paula did not release my arm. When Raphael emerged from the kitchen, she rushed to his side and he hugged her tightly, stroking her hair and murmuring soothing words in Italian.

'This is the only room that has been vandalized,' Trelawny said. 'Are you all right?'

'No, but I'll survive.' Leaning against the doorjamb, I felt a wave of despair at the sight of the broken china and shattered crystal. Our little world had been turned upside down yet again.

Paula jerked her head up and exclaimed, 'I must pick up Georgiana – now.'

'But she will be asleep, and we must contact the police—' I began.

'No!' she cut in quickly. 'I must have her with me.'

Raphael turned to me and said, 'I will send word to the *polizia* after we have Georgiana.'

Nodding, I waved them off.

After they exited, I met Trelawny's somber eyes. 'Thank goodness I had locked my Byron/Shelley letters in my desk after the incident at the Boboli Gardens. Do you think they intended to steal them?'

'Difficult to say.' He scanned the room once more, his glance halting on a book of Byron's poetry with its leather cover partially ripped away from the spine. Pages had been torn out and shredded into tiny, jagged fragments – and a knife pinned them to the floor in what appeared to be an act of rage. Leaning down, I retrieved a single page which had been left intact – it was the poem that Byron had written to me in the summer of 1816, beginning with the lines:

> There be none of Beauty's daughters
> With a magic like thee . . .

But the magic was gone.

I let the sheet flutter to the floor.

Trelawny cursed under his breath as he sifted through the books and papers. After a few minutes of hunting, he rose and turned to me with a somber expression. 'I am sorry, Claire, but it appears the Cades sketch that we left on the table is missing.'

*Dio mio.* Our last dream to escape poverty had just died.

And with it, all hope.


*Palazzo Guiccioli, Ravenna, Italy*
*July 1820*

*Allegra's story*

It was so nice to be living with my dear papa again.

Lord Byron.

When he finally sent for me, I could barely sleep until I set out from Venice. It was a long carriage ride to Ravenna – almost two days – but I did not mind because I was so excited to see him again. The sweet-faced nursemaid from England who traveled with me grew irritable by the hour because I chattered endlessly in Italian about my new home.

What would it be like?

Would I have a governess?

How long would we stay there?

She dabbed at her flushed cheeks with a handkerchief, complaining about the heat and demanding that I speak English, but I hardly remembered that language now. I spoke only Italian and that seemed to annoy her even more. But I did not care. Once we arrived and I was with my papa again, everything would be wonderful.

*La bella vita.*

When we drove up to the Palazzo Guiccioli on the Via Cavour in the late afternoon, I immediately sprang out of the carriage and beheld my new home. It was large and imposing, like all of Papa's houses, with three stories built of brownish brick and lots of green shuttered windows. So elegant.

Then I saw Papa standing in the doorway, wearing a white shirt open at the neck and black breeches.

I heard the nursemaid catch her breath from inside the carriage.

Papa always had that effect on people – men and women. Because he was so famous, they would often be awestruck in his presence. Staring and stammering. He would be polite to them, but I could tell that he was uncomfortable with such behavior, especially when they stared down at his club foot.

He was just Papa to me, the generous man who bought me silk dresses and china dolls when we lived in Venice. On rare evenings when he stayed in, he would read English poetry to me in a soft, melodious voice, even though I did not understand most of the words. Sometimes he would stop reciting and stare off into the distance with a sad look in his eyes, but he never said what was wrong.

When he moved to Ravenna, he said he would send for me – and it finally happened. He had not forgotten about me.

Running toward him, I stretched out my arms. He allowed me a brief hug, then told me to go inside while he had a servant see to my luggage.

I waved farewell to the nursemaid, but she had eyes only for Papa. He said something in English to her, dismissed the carriage driver, and then followed me into the palazzo. As I entered the foyer and scanned the rich surroundings, my eyes widened at the marble floors and gilt-edged furniture. Truly, a palace.

Then I spied Papa's cats scurrying about with two small dogs; they tumbled over each other in playful romps until the peacock appeared and began squawking. The animals scurried off and Papa laughed. After he ushered me up the stairs to the third floor, we stepped into his study – a large, high-ceilinged room lined with books on every side. I recognized the desk and furnishings *from* Venice. It felt like home.

A pretty lady with blond hair stood near the painted screen by the window; she was chatting with a young man who looked like her – both charming and amiable. When they saw me, the conversation stopped abruptly.

'This is Contessa Guiccioli and her brother, Pietro Gamba,' Papa said.

The lady inclined her head and glided over to the sofa; she patted the cushion next to her with an inviting smile, and I immediately skipped over to take my seat. '*Buongiorno*, Allegra,' she greeted me as she stroked my hair with a tender touch. She smelled like jasmine flowers.

'*Buongiorno, Contessa.*'

She then asked me about my journey, and I told her about seeing the Adriatic coast and watching the water birds feeding at the Isola d'Ariano – enchanting.

'*Si . . . incantevole*,' she agreed.

As the contessa told me about her family in Ravenna, I noted that Papa had joined Pietro and they began to converse quietly in Italian. I could not catch any of the words except *turba* and *d'apprentis*. Mob. Apprentice. It made no sense to me.

Just then, a huge and black-bearded man strode into the room. I jumped up and exclaimed, 'Tita!'

'Allegrina!' Laughing, he swept me up in his massive arms in tight embrace. Tita Falcieri was a gondolier who had become Papa's manservant. Powerful, with a booming voice, he always wore a hat with a plume of feathers and a sword in his sash. He also brought me *fritole* when we lived in Venice. I especially liked the ones stuffed with chocolate.

He put me down again and patted me on the head before he joined Papa and Pietro.

Tita was quickly drawn into their conversation – and their

voices rose in agitation. I thought I heard the word Carbonari and asked them what that meant. No one replied.

Quickly, the contessa asked me if I would like to see my new room, but I did not want to leave Papa when I had just arrived. I began to whimper and pout until he promised to read a poem to me after supper.

My happiness restored, I let the contessa take me by the hand to lead me out.

I glanced over my shoulder at Papa, but he was deep in conversation with Tita and Pietro again.

They looked worried.

# TWO

'The sense of earth and earthly things come back,
Corrosive passions, feelings, dull and low . . .'

*The Prophecy of Dante*, I, 131–132

*Florence, Italy*
*July 1873*

I was exhausted.

An aching, heavy fatigue had settled into every part of my body, and I struggled to remain awake.

Since we had returned to find my apartment at the Palazzo Cruciato vandalized, the *polizia* remained for hours questioning each of us in turn – first in Italian, then in English to make certain we understood their intent. Lieutenant Baldini, the chief of police who had visited me after Father Gianni's death, was in charge again. A young man with a serious face and polite manner, he quietly conducted his investigation, taking copious notes but making only an occasional comment. In spite of my tiredness, I found his presence quite comforting.

'*Signora* Clairmont, I apologize for keeping you so late, but I have a few more questions.' He slowly paced around my sitting room with a small notebook in hand, while I remained on the settee, Trelawny next to me. Gas lamps illuminated the room's disheveled interior with books and papers strewn on the floor along with a few broken china knickknacks.

I had not taken an inventory beyond the Cades sketch – and checking to make certain my Byron letters remained untouched.

Mr Rossetti eventually departed after giving his account of the evening, and Paula and Raphael were still in the kitchen conversing with two of Baldini's officers. Little Georgiana lay asleep on my bed, blissfully unaware of the chaotic events around her in the sweet repose of a child. How I envied her.

'Is it necessary to continue this conversation tonight?' Trelawny asked, drumming his fingers on the settee's armrest. Not known for his patience or calm temper – especially in the face of uncertainty – Trelawny grew more and more agitated. He was always the man who took charge and did not like being compliant, especially with a police officer.

'*Si.*' Baldini picked up the book of Byron's poetry that had been slashed with a knife, contemplated it for a few moments, then set it on the tea table again next to the silver filigreed inkwell that Shelley had given to me. It, too, was untouched – my treasured possession that had been a token of his friendship. I never had been able to part with it. 'The immediacy of my fact-finding may initiate a quick arrest.'

'I understand.' Blinking a few times to refocus my eyes, I continued, 'The past two weeks or so have been jarring, to say the least. After Matteo was arrested, I thought our lives would return to the uneventful days of the past, but that seems unlikely at this point.'

'*Questo dipende.*' He moved toward the fireplace, stepping around a smashed etched-glass flower vase, its contents spilled on the floor – water and crushed rose petals splattered about. 'It depends on the intruder's motivation—'

Trelawny made a scoffing sound. 'You question that? When Signora Clairmont's valuable Cades sketch seems to be the only stolen item?'

'I meant that the original goal may have been to steal your letters, but the thieves changed their plan when they could not find them quickly. It is well known around Firenze that you possess letters from the famous poet himself. But what intrigues me is how the robbers would know to look for the drawing.' Baldini's gaze came to rest on me. 'If I understand what you told me, you took possession of the sketch only recently. Who else would know about it besides your immediate family and friends?'

'I . . . I cannot say.' A slight chill had crept in, and I pulled my shawl tighter. 'I am not sure who might have known about the sketch. Mr Rossetti arrived in Florence with it more than two weeks ago, having brought it from England – until that time, his mother owned it, though it was not on display in her home. He then gave it to me that night after Matteo tried to kill me. Did you ask him if he shared the drawing's existence with anyone else?'

Baldini nodded. 'Apparently, he showed it only to his brother, Dante Gabriel – an artist himself – who was sworn to secrecy.'

'So we have no idea as to the thief's motivation . . .' I said, half to myself.

'This is a somewhat delicate inquiry, but do you believe Raphael and your niece to be completely . . . trustworthy?' Baldini's words came out haltingly, as if he were treading upon an uneven path. 'I do not mean to suggest that they deliberately engineered the theft, but perhaps one of them unwittingly mentioned the Cades drawing to a friend or neighbor in passing; the artist's name would be recognized by most Italians and might have caused an unscrupulous person to steal it.'

I mentally sorted through every person with whom Paula and Raphael regularly had contact. The carriage driver? No, he was a young man of earnest character. Our neighbors who sometimes watched Georgiana? Again – no. They were a pleasant couple with two young children of their own. The local *macellaio* – butcher? Unlikely. We had known them all for years, and none of them seemed capable of thievery.

I raised my brows at the lieutenant's suggestion. 'I assume you asked Paula and Raphael and they both denied mentioning the sketch?'

'*Si.*'

'Then I believe them.' Stifling a yawn, I felt my shoulders begin to sag.

Trelawny gestured toward me with a raised hand. 'This line of questioning is leading nowhere, and Signora Clairmont needs her rest – as do we all. Should she have anything to add, I can send word to you, but I doubt if there is anyone else in Florence who knew that Rossetti gave Claire the drawing.'

A sudden thought occurred to me, in spite of the fatigue.

*No one . . . other than possibly the man in jail – he knew everything that occurred in the city.*

'What about Matteo Ricci?' I queried. 'He might have learned about the sketch . . . and could have directed someone to steal it.'

'From prison?' Trelawny shook his head. 'A remote possibility at best, Claire.'

'I agree,' Baldini said.

'Perhaps.' Rubbing my temples, I closed my eyes briefly to summon a last wave of energy and strength during this endless night. 'This may sound mad, but I want to come by the police station tomorrow to talk with him.'

The two men drew in a collective breath.

'Absolutely not.' Trelawny stared down at me as if I had, indeed, lost my mind.

'Signora, perhaps I did not hear you correctly,' Baldini began. 'You want to visit the man who threatened to kill you?'

Glancing back and forth between them, I hesitated – not because I doubted myself but, rather, I knew they both were already gauging whether or not to take my request seriously, and I was marshaling my defenses. I had not passed a lifetime in the company of men without learning a lesson or two about playing upon their sympathies. The delicate art of persuasion was sometimes a woman's best tool. 'I may be a bit foggy at this hour, but I think that Matteo might know about the stolen sketch – even you, Lieutenant, said that he probably has connections with thievery rings in Florence. And who better than I to ask him? Unlike the *polizia*, I am no threat to him since I am simply a . . . harmless woman.'

Baldini managed a small smile. 'Any man who would think that is a fool.'

'You are not actually considering her request?' Trelawny exclaimed in disbelief. 'Prison is no place for a lady.'

'*Lei è molto persuasiva* – I may consider it,' he said shortly. 'But I, too, am tired and want to consider the matter carefully. For now, I shall take my leave and will send a note tomorrow morning with my decision.' The lieutenant gave a short bow and then called for his officers who were still in the kitchen.

Trelawny showed them out, and I heard some hushed, urgent debate near the front door. He was trying one more time to influence Baldini's decision. Their voices rose slightly in volume for a few minutes, but from the force of Trelawny's slammed door behind them and succinct curse that followed, I assumed that my old friend had not prevailed.

Still swearing under his breath, Trelawny strolled back into the sitting room. 'I suppose there is nothing else I can say to dissuade you.'

'No.'

'I must remind you that Matteo is a criminal and has committed a murder.' His tone hardened. 'I have lived every day of my life with the guilt of my lies, but I could not go on if anything happened to you or your family.' His eyes darkened with emotion as he pleaded for caution.

My heart stirred slightly from his appeal, though it seemed a little too late in coming to express such devotion. 'Let me do this – you can accompany me to the jail, should Baldini grant my request, and I will not leave your sight.'

Trelawny glanced down and sighed heavily. 'You are decided on this course?'

'I am.'

His head tilted upward again, staring forward. 'Then I shall help you – with reservations, for certain.'

But his warnings had struck a chord inside; I would remain vigilant. There were too many secrets that had swirled around me over the last two weeks, which had proved to be hiding evil intent. And more could follow.

Somewhat revived after a short night's sleep, I took breakfast with Paula and Raphael in our kitchen while Georgiana skipped around the room, humming to herself. A servant had appeared earlier with a note from Baldini for me, but I kept the news to myself until Paula set out the breakfast. Then I casually mentioned that I had proposed to visit Matteo in prison and just received word that Lieutenant Baldini agreed. Not surprisingly, they reacted with a mixture of alarm and disbelief. Even though Trelawny had acquiesced (albeit reluctantly) to my decision to see Matteo, they raised heated and passionate pleas for me to reconsider my plan – along with warnings about how dank, unhealthy prisons could be deadly for a woman of advanced age (I did not need to hear *that*).

'It is also unseemly.' Paula grimaced. 'A lady would never be seen in such a place.'

'Or put herself in proximity to criminals,' Raphael added.

They exchanged glances from where they sat across the old wooden table, adorned with a rough, linen tablecloth and vase of white roses which Trelawny had given to me. Paula and Raphael sat side by side, close and united in their concern. I did not doubt they had my best interests at heart, but I had already made up my mind and no one would dissuade me.

Calmly, I buttered my bread and sipped my morning cappuccino, letting them continue as I focused on Georgiana's joyful, springy steps as she launched into her favorite *filastrocca* – a nursery rhyme that included clapping as she chanted '*Batta le manine.*'

'Aunt Claire, are you paying attention to us?' Paula demanded, her light-blue eyes clouded with uneasiness as she admonished Georgiana to quiet down. 'I cannot believe that you would even consider something so reckless. Just think what could happen if Matteo tried to harm you again? He has already murdered once when he stabbed poor Father Gianni, and that was at the Medici Chapel – a very public place. What do you think could happen in a prison where you will be locked away from the world?'

'Not to worry, my dear; Trelawny will be with me.' I handed a small piece of bread to Georgiana who nibbled away, resuming her dance.

'But he is *molto anziano*,' Raphael chimed in, shaking his head. 'How can a man protect you at his . . . age?'

Affronted, I stiffened my shoulders. 'He is hardly in his dotage – and was, I remind you, a fearless soldier in several wars—'

'That was years ago, Aunt,' Paula interjected in a firm voice. 'You forget that he is not the same person that you knew in your youth.'

'I agree, but his strength is undiminished.' Or so I wanted to believe.

Georgiana began singing more loudly, and my niece turned toward her and hissed, '*Silenzio!*' She immediately halted, her features cast down with dismay, and I pulled Georgiana on to my lap in a reassuring embrace.

'I appreciate that both of you care so deeply about my well-being, but I must be guided by what I think is best.' My voice was gentle but firm. 'I will take all necessary precautions, Trelawny and Lieutenant Baldini will be with me, and I promise not to do anything foolish that might antagonize Matteo. But I must know if he has some piece of information that could help us solve the thievery that occurred last night. It is possible, given his long-standing criminal activities. That Cades drawing meant more to me than I can say – and not just because it was part of my past; its sale would help considerably to alleviate our poverty.' I gestured at the bare walls and empty shelves around us.

Paula picked at a loose thread in the tablecloth. 'I know our financial state leaves much to be desired, but I would rather scrape along than have you put yourself at risk of injury.'

'Oh, my dear, you shall not be rid of me so easily – I promise.' Dropping a light kiss on Georgiana's head, I added, 'Would you feel better if Raphael came along?'

'Perhaps.'

Raphael's face lit with pride. 'I shall guard her well, trust me.'

Paula's frown lightened somewhat, and I clasped her hand as if to remind her that he had more than proven himself at the Pitti Palace when he had fought with Matteo and saved us from being shot.

And he loved her.

Indeed, he was the type of man who I had always hoped would love Paula: someone to be counted on when events seemed most dire. He might not have wealth, but he possessed character – and I had come to believe that trait was more desirable than any other in life.

'I suppose that I must agree – on the condition that Raphael accompanies you,' Paula finally said, handing Georgiana a slice of buttered bread as a peace offering. 'Where is Matteo being held?'

'I believe Baldini told me . . . Le Murate,' I said.

Raphael gasped. 'That is where they hold political prisoners – ruffians and villains. A hellish place.'

'*Murate?* Does that not mean "walled up"?' Paula queried. 'A fitting name for a jail.'

'It was not originally a prison.' Raphael took on a thoughtful air as he brushed his fingers across the rose petals. 'It was a convent built in the 1400s – the Santissima Annunziata alle Murate and Santa Caterina. The nuns who resided there chose the cloistered life, so they were *murate* – walled up. Some believe they lived a holy existence, but many of the nuns were said to have gone mad with the isolation – haunted souls within the stone walls.'

'How awful.' My arms tightened around Georgiana as if to protect her from such a fate. 'What happened to the nuns?'

'They were evicted when Napoleon conquered *Italia*. He confiscated the convent and sold all the gold artifacts to pay for his warmongering. By that time, there were only a handful of nuns left who lived there, and they scattered to the winds after they were turned out, never to be heard from again,' Raphael said on a sorrowful note. 'Later, before Risorgimento, political prisoners were held there . . . and tortured. More men will be walled up there in the future, no doubt. Those who follow the shadowy road of crime will find a home there, never to be seen again.'

Paula touched his cheek with a soft caress. 'Thank God that was not your fate, my love.'

She avoided referring directly to his misspent adolescence, but the unspoken reference lingered in the silence. Raphael had lived hand to mouth as a child of deceased parents, not sure where his next meal would be found. I could only guess what he had to do to survive, although he had never related more than the barest details to me.

He took her hand and buried a kiss in the palm. 'I moved into the light when I met you, Paula. No more darkness.'

'Yes, indeed – Paula's love has transformed you,' I added. 'The men of Le Murate may also be those who can be redeemed and restored to the same place where you are now, Raphael.'

'Not Matteo.' He frowned. 'There is nothing good in him – perhaps there never was. No, he is vile to the core.'

Paula visibly shuddered, then glanced at me. 'Are you sure that you want to go there, Aunt? It sounds like a horrible place, scarcely fit for a gentleman, much less a lady.'

'I shall be fine, I assure you.'

My niece, her pale and beautiful face still filled with doubt, finally gave in with a short nod.

By early afternoon, I was seated in our small open carriage, which Raphael expertly steered through the narrow, crooked streets of Florence. With only my parasol as a shield from the sun, I leaned back against the worn brocade cushions, hardly noticing the impact of its wheels thumping on the uneven stones. I was too distracted at the prospect of speaking with Matteo, our seemingly kindly landlord who, as I had learned only recently, had a secret criminal life in Florence.

The hidden alleyways and shady corners where brutality flourished.

A tiny puff of breeze fluttered against the bare skin of my arms as we crossed the Ponte Vecchio, but it dissipated the moment we entered the crowded square on the other side of the Arno River. Fanning myself, I traced the modest neckline of my best light-green muslin dress, lingering over my mother's gold locket, which I had donned to give me strength. And for the hundredth time, on this day of all days, I wished fervently to have known the identity of my father who gave it to her.

She never spoke of him, and I never asked.

But I could not think of them today because I had to keep my wits focused on the task ahead at Le Murate. The words echoed through my mind, soft and melodic. So strange how the Italian language could make even a sinister prison sound like a soulful paradise.

People already swarmed around the Uffizi Palace, speaking in various languages as they hurried toward the gallery that housed some of Italy's greatest artists – all eager to behold the magnificent paintings of Botticelli and Da Vinci.

Raphael turned down the Via Ghibellina and, after a few more blocks, halted the carriage in front of Le Murate – a grim, multi-storied structure. Built of rough, blanched stone, its high, forbidding walls were dotted with barred windows. No possibility of escape; these portals were fashioned to keep prisoners inside and hope locked outside.

Trelawny and Baldini stood under an archway in front of two massive wooden doors; both men wore black jackets and somber expressions. As I scanned the prison's bleak exterior, I felt a moment's hesitation. Had I made a mistake in coming here? Was it more dangerous than I had realized? Before I could change my mind, Raphael halted the carriage and Trelawny moved forward to assist me.

*I could not turn back now.*

Trelawny grasped my elbow as I stepped out of the carriage, whispering, 'You do not have to see him yourself; Baldini and I can question Matteo while you listen outside his cell.'

*A tempting offer – but no.* 'I . . . I think a woman's touch might work better with someone like Matteo.'

'He deserves to be hanged.' Trelawny gave a short, scoffing exclamation. 'I only wish that I could be there to watch.'

'There will be none of that talk,' Lieutenant Baldini cut in with a warning note in his voice. 'Our Italian laws will dispense justice as it is due. Even though Matteo confessed to murder, he will be given a fair trial and a judge's sentence. I must remind you that he may not be involved in the second crime at all since he was here at Le Murate when your apartment was vandalized last night. This visit is a courtesy to you as a guest in our country.'

'Certainly.' I could not disagree with the young lieutenant; this was probably a fool's errand, but if there was a chance that Matteo had any connection to the theft of the obelisk sketch, I had to give it a try. 'We are most appreciative of your generosity.'

I told Raphael that I would be finished in half an hour. He agreed with a warning nod in Trelawny's direction before he urged the horse forward.

'I believe Raphael would slit my throat if I allowed anything to happen to you,' Trelawny said matter-of-factly as he escorted me toward the entrance. 'But he need not worry – I will have my eye on Matteo the whole time. You are quite safe.'

Feeling somewhat reassured, I slipped my arm through Trelawny's as I readied myself for what awaited us. Then Baldini pushed against one of the doors, which made a loud creaking sound as it opened slowly, almost like a low-pitched moan of unheard voices and lost memories.

Once we were inside, the air took on a damp and cool

quality, like the moss-lined walkways near the Arno River – a relief from the heat, but too clammy for comfort. An elderly man with thin shoulders and a craggy face was stationed at a small table. As we drew near, he held out a quill. '*Il nome?*'

Trelawny and I signed our names in a large book and moved on.

Baldini led us down a soundless corridor lined with identical wooden doors on either side; each one had an iron bar stretched across the middle section that fit into a large, sturdy lock. Most of the doors stood open, bars up . . . waiting for the men that would be brought here to spend their days shut away from society. Waiting for the last march out of the daylight into darkness. Waiting for the end of all dreams.

It made me remember another time and place when I had visited a prison.

Very different, but no less harsh.

During that summer of 1816, I secretly met Byron at Castle Chillon on Lake Geneva. He had sailed there with Shelley to see the abandoned fortress that once held François Bonivard – a religious reformer who spent seven years chained to a stone pillar before he was liberated. I had been filled with romantic ideas of meeting my lover in that ancient citadel to tell him I was expecting his child. *So naïve.* When I surprised Byron in the dungeon and revealed my news, it did not go as I had planned . . . He made it clear that marriage was not an option. I was so upset that I tumbled down the stairs, although I always believed someone had shoved me. Perhaps it had been di Breme's servant – I do not know. It was so long ago . . .

But I could see the castle in my mind's eye and hear the lines from Byron's poem to honor Bonivard, 'The Prisoner of Chillon':

> Dim with a dull imprison'd ray,
> A sunbeam which hath lost its way,
> And through the crevice and the cleft
> Of the thick wall is fallen and left . . .

Oddly, as I remembered those lines, it brought me back to the present and somehow made Le Murate more bearable, remembering that Bonivard had been freed. The sun could penetrate even the most dismal place.

'We have few "residents" since they are still renovating the buildings,' Baldini was saying as our footsteps echoed on the stone floor. 'But I expect that Le Murate will fill quickly; there is never a scarcity of criminals.'

I said nothing, still striving to rein in my memories.

Once we reached the end of the hallway, we climbed steep, narrow stairs to the second floor. It, too, echoed with emptiness. Then Baldini led us through an archway and pointed at a much larger wooden door than the ones downstairs. 'This is the cell that once housed political dissidents during the Risorgimento – one of few that still is habitable.'

'Too good for a rogue like him,' Trelawny muttered.

'Perhaps, but if we do not treat men humanely, then we are no better that the prisoners that we prosecute.' Baldini produced a key and unlocked the iron bar, swinging it upwards in one smooth motion. 'Matteo is expecting you both.'

As Baldini unlatched the door, he turned to me with an unreadable expression in his eyes. 'I would not expect much from him. There seems to be very little empathy left in him now that the façade of his life has been stripped away. He may seem civil on the surface, but that is mere pretense.' He paused. 'I shall return in thirty minutes.'

After he left, I steeled myself for the chamber's foul conditions and the even more repugnant sight of Matteo as we entered, Trelawny at my elbow. But, surprisingly, the small room had clean, white walls, neatly arranged furniture, and even a portrait of a Tuscan villa at sunset hanging near the iron-barred window. Not lavish by any means, but not filthy either. Matteo was seated at a small, plain desk reading a book with the air of a gentleman in his study.

Irritation flooded through me as I beheld him lounging so pleasantly after he had viciously stabbed my dear friend, Father Gianni. But he had an ancient family name and some political connections, which I supposed afforded some degree of creature comforts.

'Are you surprised to see me not living in squalor, Signora Clairmont?' Matteo asked without looking up as he turned a page.

'Perhaps "surprised" is not the word I would use.' I heard the edge in my voice; it held the sharpness of a thin blade cutting through paper. 'But men like you always seem to find a way to enjoy the comforts that you have possessed as a Florentine of rank and station.'

'Until the noose is placed around your neck,' Trelawny spat out. 'I have seen many villains end like that, and it is a painful death, believe me . . .'

'Edward, enough.' I might resent Matteo's amenities, but I did not want to imagine his agony at the end of a rope. That type of brutal revenge held no attraction for me in spite of the justness of the punishment.

'Please, sit.' He gestured toward two high-backed chairs, upholstered in faded red velvet.

I complied, but Trelawny remained standing, positioned behind me.

'Finally, you have found a *cavaliere* who seems a worthy companion for you,' Matteo commented as he closed his book, his glance flitting over both of us with a disagreeable gleam. 'I always wondered why you lived without a protector in *Firenze* with only your niece and her daughter; even now, you possess the type of charms that a man would find attractive. You must have been quite beautiful when young – *la bella figura*, with the fiery looks of our Italian clime.'

Trelawny bristled, and I cut in quickly, 'That was many years ago, and I will remind you that I am a respectable, if somewhat . . . middle-aged English woman.'

'Of course.' Smiling, he held up the book and my breath caught in my throat as I saw the title.

*The Prophecy of Dante.*

Byron's poem, written during his years in Ravenna – a lyrical tribute to the beloved Italian poet. He thought it was his best work, but I could never bring myself to read it since it was dedicated to his last mistress, Teresa Guiccioli – the 'Lady . . . in the pride of Beauty and Youth,' as he described her.

'I find your poet's theme of being exiled appeals to me right now.' He gave a short, ironic laugh. 'Like Dante, I have been disowned by everyone, reviled by one and all, so I shall expect no mercy at my trial. I know that.'

Shifting with discomfort, I eyed the book's cover with Byron's name blazoned across the upper half in large gold cursive script. I knew he had written it in 1821 when he lived in Ravenna with Teresa – a wealthy, beautiful, young Italian woman who was also married; she was the perfect combination for Byron's last liaison, until she left her husband to live openly with the poet as her lover. No more furtive meetings in the lush, romantic pine forests – just the domestic messiness of being a *cavaliere servente*. I had heard all about it from Shelley when he, Mary, and I lived in Pisa on the other coast of Italy at the same time. Mary had been shocked at Byron's *ménage à trois*, but I had not. He made women forget all sense and reason – and I included myself in this coterie. I would have followed him anywhere as long as I had Allegra with me.

*Ah . . . I missed the passion of my youth.*

'You deserve the fate that awaits you, sir.' Trelawny stressed the last word with a sneer. 'Anyone who would kill a man of God has no right to live.'

'*Forse.*' Matteo shrugged. 'I do not pretend to be other than the man I am, flawed and corrupt, but Father Gianni may not have been the saint that most Florentines believed him to be—'

'How dare you vilify the dead!' I exclaimed. 'Father Gianni was the kindest person I have ever met. His entire life was devoted to his parishioners – helping even those who were some of the worst sinners. You have no right to say such things about him.'

Glancing at me dispassionately, his crooked index finger tapped the book cover. 'You forget, Signora Clairmont, that I have known him all of my life . . . even before he took on the holy robes. We grew up together and, as a young man, he shared my early dissolute years, but he learned how to pretend at righteousness.'

'You lie.' I glared at him, affronted at the slander.

But Matteo did not even flinch. 'What is the point in lying? I am staring my own death in the face and have no desire to add to my sins. I am telling you the truth: Father Gianni was not all that he seemed.' The tapping stopped.

*No.*

*It could not be true.*

And yet . . . something inside of me shifted slightly as I watched Matteo's calm demeanor remain unchanged in spite of my accusations. 'Is this why you agreed to see me? So you could demean Father Gianni's memory? For God's sake, have you not done enough by taking his life?'

He paused, then continued, 'I wanted you to know that I was not the only evil man at the Basilica di San Lorenzo that day when you spoke to Father Gianni. Many deceptions surrounded that meeting. It is true that I wanted your letters from the English poets; they would have fetched a large sum, and I would have done anything to obtain them. But Father Gianni would have sold his soul to keep some parts of the letters hidden. Both of us stood before God that day with something to hide, and we will answer for our sins.'

'You are the only one who will answer for his sins,' I said, but doubts began to creep into my mind – tiny glimmers of mistrust. I refused to give in wholly to it. I *would* not. 'Even if Father Gianni had a past he wished to hide, that is hardly the same as theft and murder.'

'Can you be so sure?'

'Enough of this nonsense!' Trelawny circled around my chair and stood in front of Matteo, looking down at him with dismissive contempt, as if he were already among the dead. 'We came here to find out whether you were involved in vandalizing Signora Clairmont's apartment last night. A very valuable drawing was stolen – one that held great sentiment for her.'

He raised a brow. 'How could I have done such a deed when I was imprisoned here? In case you have not noticed, the walls of Le Murate are thick and impenetrable.'

'You did not answer my question,' Trelawny pressed, his hands clenched at his sides. 'And I hardly believe that your network of thieves and criminals does not extend beyond this prison.'

'You overestimate my influence, Signor.'

'Not likely.'

Just then, I heard footsteps coming down the corridor outside, and I realized that our time was almost up. Leaning forward, I continued, 'Lieutenant Baldini is returning, so I implore you to tell me if you know who took my drawing. If it is returned, I could sell it and would be able to give Paula and Georgiana a future beyond our present poverty.'

His glance fastened on my mother's gold locket. 'You might consider selling that piece of jewelry; it is quite unusual and might be worth something – should you want to part with it.'

'Never.' I drew back, covering it with my hand. 'My father gave it to my mother, so it is very precious to me – more than anything that I own.'

'A family heirloom?' His eyes gleamed – ever greedy.

'Yes – and the last link to my parents.'

'Of course.' Matteo stared at me for a few seconds, then switched to rapid-fire Italian as he slipped an intricately carved ivory bookmark out of Byron's poetry volume. 'In that spirit, take this – it is my gift to make up for the ill that I have done to you, though I know nothing about the theft of your sketch. I could have sold it many times over but could not bring myself to do so since my own deceased father gave it to me. He brought it back from a trip to India, so it has some value.' He handed it to me as he lowered his voice. 'I have lived a sinful life, but that is between God and me. I told the truth about the priest – he knew more than he revealed to you about your daughter and what happened to her. Trust no one, Signora Clairmont. Even now, there are powerful people who want to hide what happened in Ravenna all those years ago—'

'How would you know that?' I demanded, taken aback by what he seemed to know – and what he seemed to suggest about Father Gianni.

'What did he say?' Trelawny exclaimed. 'I cannot follow his Italian.'

Baldini cleared his throat; he stood in the doorway of the prison cell. 'Your time is up; you must leave now.'

*No! Let him finish*, I exclaimed inside.

Fighting to control my frustration, I slipped the bookmark in my bag as I rose from the chair. 'Perhaps we could speak another time.' I stressed the last words.

'That is not possible,' Baldini said, gesturing for us to exit the cell. 'I just received orders that Matteo will be transferred immediately to Rome for trial.'

*I shall never see him again – or find out what else he knows.* My throat ached in defeat.

'Come away, Claire.' Trelawny grasped my arm. 'There is nothing more for you here.' He drew me toward the doorway, and I took one last glance over my shoulder at Matteo before we exited.

'*Addio,* Signora.' Matteo folded his hands in a prayer position as a sly smile spread across his face, telling me he knew more than he had just revealed. In that moment, I felt scant pity for him and his descent from a rich and opulent life to a bleak, cramped space of a jail cell. He would die a criminal's death.

A wretched last act, but perhaps well deserved.

Baldini shut the door behind us, thumped down the iron bar, and locked the dead bolt. Then he placed the key in his jacket's breast pocket. 'I assume he denied being involved in the vandalism of your apartment.'

I nodded.

'Did you believe him?' he queried.

Wavering, I finally answered evasively, 'He seemed to be making peace with his life – or at least acknowledging his sins.'

'People say many things when driven by desperation.' Trelawny peered up and down the deserted corridor, always on alert. 'Like Doctor Faustus, that type of man will always seek forgiveness in the eleventh hour to save his soul, but it is only because he faces the gaping pit of hell. Let him be damned.'

'I fear that is so.' Pulling the drawstrings of my bag tightly closed, I slipped them around my wrist.

'Did Matteo say anything else to you?' Baldini inquired as we strolled down the hallway toward the stairs.

'Nothing of significance . . .' Biting my lip, I added, 'He said something in Italian, but I could not catch all of it since he spoke so quickly.'

Trelawny stiffened – he knew my Italian was impeccable.

Without further questions, the lieutenant escorted us

downstairs and then out of the entranceway. As we emerged from Le Murate, the midday heat bore down with a breathless intensity, and I was grateful that Raphael had already pulled up the carriage; he sat in the driver's seat, leaning forward with the horse reins in hand. Trelawny helped me on to the seat and took his place beside me.

'I shall come by tomorrow afternoon,' Baldini promised with an enigmatic look. 'Just in case you remember anything else.'

Extending my hand to him, I smiled. 'I look forward to it.'

Raphael flicked the crop and the horse took off at a brisk pace. Once we were out of sight, Trelawny turned to me. 'What exactly did Matteo say to you?'

I related Matteo's accusations against Father Gianni as we made our way through the crowded midday streets. Trelawny said little in response as the carriage creaked and groaned its way across the Ponte Vecchio and down the Via Romana until we halted outside the Palazzo Cruciato.

Trelawny helped me descend the carriage steps and finally spoke: 'We must take back the carriage before the horse becomes overheated. You need to rest—'

'But—'

'Please, do this for me.' He waited until I acquiesced, then he climbed on to the seat next to Raphael. 'We shall not be long.'

I watched them drive off and then made my way upstairs.

As soon as I entered the apartment, Paula appeared and began fussing over me. 'Aunt Claire, what happened? You were gone so long that I grew worried . . . This hot weather cannot be good for someone of your age.'

'I am fine – really.' Removing my bonnet, I decided to ignore the comment about my advanced years. At times, I felt as if my niece considered me as decrepit as the aging furniture in our rented apartment.

'While you were gone, I straightened the mess from last night and found nothing else missing besides the sketch . . . at least as far as I could tell.' She ushered me into the sitting room and on to my favorite wingback chair. 'I want to hear everything about your visit with Matteo, but first I have to retrieve Georgiana. Perhaps you can rest until I return.' She did not phrase it as a question.

'Of course. Thank you for attending to our apartment, my dear.' Leaning back, I settled into the soft cushion. 'I am a bit tired, but I promise to fill you in later over a nice cup of tea.'

She hugged me tightly and then let herself out.

After I heard Paula exit and close the door behind her, I immediately straightened, then reached inside my bag to retrieve the bookmark that Matteo had given to me. How ironic that it had been placed inside his copy of *The Prophecy of Dante* – the poem that Byron had written at the suggestion of my rival for his affections: Teresa Guiccioli. It had not been a hugely popular poem in England, and it had received only modest acclaim in Italy – both of which facts pleased me since it was dedicated to his Italian mistress.

Even now, after all these years, the thought of another woman as Byron's muse caused a dull ache in my heart, blunted somewhat by the distance of time, but there nonetheless. A jealous echo that stretched through the years, growing ever fainter with each stage of my life, but not completely gone. Still with the power to taunt me.

We each had our time with him, forever fixed by the verse that he had written to us – she as Beatrice to his Dante, and I as 'Beauty's daughter.'

And what of Matteo's comments about Father Gianni? Had the priest been conspiring to obtain Byron's letters for himself? If so, why? All I knew for certain is that whatever happened in Ravenna all those years ago held the missing pieces to the puzzle of Allegra's fate.

I knew what I had to do.

Slowly, I walked into my room, retrieved Bryon's lost Ravenna memoir from my desk, and began to read . . .


*Palazzo Guiccioli, Ravenna, Italy*
*December 7, 1820*

*La Mia Confessione . . .*

*I was ready to begin my life anew.*
*Poised for change in the way a man can do only when he*

*has exhausted the senses and delved into the inner realms of utter depravity . . . all the nights in Venice where women came to me as the famous poet, flesh met flesh, but it never satisfied. Afterwards, I would slide into the cold canal water to cleanse myself but found only dank filth that permeated my skin with more grime – an 'oyster with no pearl.' It took me months and months of seeking the beauteous gem before I realized the shell of this Sea-Sodom on the Adriatic held only emptiness for me. Pain taught me truly how to feel beyond the body. It gave me my soul back.*

*It will soon be Christmas – the one-year anniversary since I, George Gordon, Lord Byron, first came to Ravenna. From the moment I entered the Porta Adriana's marble archway during the city's annual celebration of the Corpus Domini, I realized that I was fated to come to this ancient city. Just outside the gate, I waited until the procession passed, watching priests wave their incense as they chanted prayers of salvation, and young girls pacing behind in white dresses and bejeweled headdresses.*

*Ravenna.*

*Once the westernmost outpost of the Byzantine empire – city of light in the Dark Ages, where one empire ended and another began.*

*A fitting place to find my purpose anew.*

*After all the years of creating heroes in my poetry – Childe Harold and Manfred – men who aspired beyond their mortal limits, perhaps now I could aspire to be one.*

*My last journal was written in 1813 when I wrote that 'no one should be a rhymer who could be anything better' – it was true then, and it is true now. In my youth, I thought to have a career in parliament and transform the country toward a true republic – to be a leader in truth and honor such as the great Washington. Not a dictator but a 'First Man' of the people. Instead, I became a poet, and all political ambitions of creating a new England were cast aside into the dustbin of lost dreams. What an ironic twist of fate – especially after the rise and fall of Napoleon. Europe reverted to the same old, decayed systems of kings and fools.*

*And I decided to live as if nothing mattered.*

*I hurt those whom I loved the most, left England in disgrace, and became the most dissolute of beings. Eventually, it seemed pointless even to entertain the notion that I could ever be more than the wretch I had become . . . until I arrived in Ravenna.*

*I found love again.*

*I found inspiration to write again.*

*And I became a revolutionary in deed as well as word with the Carbonari – the freedom fighters who were trying to unify* Italia.

*Honor and glory may not have eluded me after all . . .*

*I am not certain how all of this will end, so I am keeping a record of my activities in Ravenna, which I will entrust to Angelo Mengaldo – he will make certain that it reaches the right hands in England. If the worst happens and I do not survive, at least there will be some sort of record of my role in this revolution, a testament that I tried to overthrow the Austrian oppressors of Romagna.*

*My belief in liberty has driven me to these actions, and I do not regret what I have done.*

Freedom.

Italia *deserves to be free, and I am willing to give my life for that freedom.*

*How did I come to fight for this great cause? Revolution had not been my intent when I moved here, but fate conspired to send me north to Dante's world.*

Mi amore. *Teresa Guiccioli. My last love.*

*My life in exile seemed empty without a true companion of the heart. I now intend to live in strictest adultery. Teresa knows how to be pleasing in every setting and has a family that live and breathe revolt – an irresistible combination.*

*And what of Claire, my daughter's mother?*

*With all the secrecy and passionate talk of revolution, I could almost forget the wrong that I have done to her. Almost. But I miss her fire and light. Her fearlessness had enthralled me from the moment we met in London, and then later in Geneva, but it was too dangerous to have her in my life.*

*Political change was coming . . . it promised to be violent and savage.*

*For now, I keep rifles and ammunition hidden in my study*

*at the Palazzo Guiccioli. Teresa's younger brother, Pietro, had smuggled in the firearms last night with a friend, knowing it would be the last place that the* polizia *would look for them – the room where I was composing* The Prophecy of Dante – *my homage to the great Italian poet.*

*I had heard only vague rumors of the Carbonari before I arrived in Ravenna from fellow poet, Ludovico di Breme, who, sadly, died six months ago. Some said they were an offshoot of the Freemasons, much like the Bavarian Illuminati, with their lodges and ancient rituals. But I found them more like frame-breakers in northern England, driven to desperate measures because of their oppression. They wanted equality and independence, so I joined them, believing their cause would be my chance of atonement.*

*Once I had become a trusted ally, Pietro and his father, Count Gamba, took me, blindfolded, to their lodge and inducted me into their secret society. During the ceremony, a Grand Master made me take an oath with two axes across my chest; when I swore my loyalty, the blindfold was removed as I saw the 'truth' of the brotherhood. The axes symbolized that arms would be raised against me if I betrayed them, but I had no intention of ever playing Judas.*

*Weeks later, I was placed in charge of my own regiment, called a* turba.

*Even as I write these words, I am somewhat amused by the fact that I have become an aging idealist, writing* The Prophecy of Dante *even as I compose cynical new cantos of* Don Juan. *High-minded grandeur and farcical absurdity. But those are the contradictions of my nature. I live in sin with a married woman and long for my lost love, Claire.*

*No one could know how much I still thought of her, still dreamed about the passionate union that produced our daughter.*

*Allegra – my love child.*

Mia cucciola.

*Since arriving in Ravenna, Allegra has become close to Teresa – calling her* mammina, *a fact that would have broken Claire's heart. But I wanted my daughter to forget her real mother; it was safer that way. It cut into my heart as well, but I had no other choice.*

*No more – no more – Oh! never more on me*
*The freshness of the heart can fall like dew,*
*Which out of all the lovely things we see*
*Extracts emotions beautiful and new,*
*Hived in our bosoms like the bag o' the bee:*
*Think'st thou the honey with those objects grew?*
*Alas! 'twas not in them, but in thy power*
*To double even the sweetness of a flower.*

*When I wrote those lines in* Don Juan, *I thought it unlikely that I would ever feel passionately committed to anything again, but this revolution has lifted me out of the dark waters of Venice into the light of hope.*

*At one time, Shelley had tried to make me believe in the power of nature to inspire humanity to create a world of beauty and perfection, but I could never accept his hopeful view of mankind. Truly, he was a much-maligned social reformer. Never willing to compromise, Shelley had paid dearly for his principles.*

*As I no doubt would, too.*

*But I would risk it for Italy's and Allegra's future.*

*If only the world could see me now as the champion of the oppressed, they might not treat me so unkindly.*

*Later that evening . . .*

*It has begun.*

*While I sat in my study with Allegra after dinner, I lapsed into a waking dream . . . and heard the sound of an organ playing a vaguely familiar song in the streets below. My ears strained to hear the melody, and I realized that it was a waltz that I had heard hundreds of times during the London season of 1812 when I was lionized by one and all after publishing* Childe Harold; *it was the turning point in my life when I shifted from wanting to be a man of action to accepting the role as a man of society.*

*I achieved fame but lost a part of myself.*

*Quietly, I eased Allegra out of my embrace and limped hurriedly down the marble stairs, then out of the front door into the narrow, snow-covered street. The organ player was already almost at the end of Via Cavour, his bent figure pausing with a brief backward glance before he disappeared in the shower of snowflakes. For a few moments, I could still hear the waltz echoing down the street, and images of dancers swirled around me in a blur of silk dresses and elegant suits. Moving gracefully to the music's lyrical flow. Laughing in the candlelight. Clapping as the waltz ended.*

*Emotion welled up inside of me at everything that I had left behind in England. All that I was . . .*

*Then one man stopped dancing and looked at me with haunted, dark eyes. He broke away from the dancers and slowly moved toward me with an unsteady gait. Gradually, the other figures faded away and I became aware that the lone man stumbling through the snow was real – a young soldier in uniform.*

*'Buonanotte.' I extended my hand, but he knocked it aside and fell against me, blood trickling from one side of his mouth in a reed-thin red line.*

*In spite of my best efforts to hold him up, he fell on to the street with a groan of pain as he hit the hard stones beneath the layer of snow. Kneeling next to him, I saw a widening red stain on his jacket, and I realized he had been shot.*

*Trembling, he murmured something under his breath that I could not decipher. He motioned me closer and, as I leaned in, I heard him hiss only one word:*

Assassino.

# THREE

'The storms yet sleep, the clouds still keep their station . . .'

*The Prophecy of Dante*, II, 40

*Florence, Italy*
*July 1873*

Slowly, I removed my spectacles and leaned back against the headrest of my chair at the Palazzo Cruciato. In spite of the open windows in my parlor, the air had grown warm and stuffy in the afternoon heat. Languid and sticky. But I felt somewhat revived after reading the journal entry. It bore out Trelawny's story: there *had* been danger all around Ravenna in 1821 with the shadows of revolution in every corner of the city – and Byron lay at the center of it with his Carbonari activities. The shooting of a soldier outside the Palazzo Guiccioli seemed a touchstone of the erupting violence of the time.

Allegra *had* been in peril.

I never thought I would accept the wisdom of placing our daughter in the convent at Bagnacavallo, but it may have been a prudent move after all.

Closing my eyes briefly, I let that knowledge seep into my thoughts. After absorbing Byron's recollections in his memoir, I could no longer doubt that he had tender feelings toward Allegra – and me. It did not even give me pause to read that Allegra called Teresa her *mammina*: I had known it at the time because Shelley had told me after he visited Byron in Ravenna. Back then, it had hurt me deeply to think my own daughter had replaced me with another woman in the role of mother, but I had shouldered that burden along with everything else when I gave her up.

Byron's words spoke to me across the stretch of time and had lessened some of the sting of my loss – he knew the depth of my sacrifice. A small thing perhaps, but not to a mother who never really had a sense of her lover as a father. I never asked for more from him, nor did he offer it.

But at the center of his *confessione* lay the lonely exile who had joined the Carbonari to find some type of atonement. That aspiring heroic side of him was unknown to me. During the summer in Geneva in 1816, he was bitter and cynical, desperate to forget about his disgrace in England, without any real allegiance to anyone or anything. I had loved him, but he had no lasting love to give me. Something had died inside of him when he became an exile, but I did not fully understand it at the time.

Like Trelawny, had I ever known Byron at all?

Did anyone?

He was an easy man to love, but an impossible one to know – and fame had made him wary. I recalled how spying, prying eyes followed his every move in Geneva, hoping to catch a glimpse of the great poet – and Shelley, Mary, and me. Tourists haunted us, gossiped incessantly, and descended even as low as to spread rumors that they had seen our undergarments hanging outside Byron's villa. My current state of obscurity as an aging survivor gave me a veil of invisibility, which Byron never knew again until the day he died.

In my mind's eye, I could imagine Byron standing here, slim and handsome as he was when I knew him, with that ironic twist to his mouth as if to say, 'See, Claire, I was not the villain that you took me for . . . I was simply a man.' Tears misted my eyes. If I had known all of this, perhaps my later feelings toward him would have been so different: full of love and compassion, instead of anger and regret.

*If only . . .*

But I had a chance now to make things right. Everything had been put in motion when Michael Rossetti came to Florence just over two weeks ago to purchase my Byron/Shelley letters, when I found out that my daughter had not died in the convent, and when my priest, Father Gianni, had been killed at the Basilica di San Lorenzo by Matteo. I thought

Father Gianni was my true friend, but Matteo had confessed a very different portrait of the priest who had seemed to me to be nothing but a sincere, holy man of the Church.

Was it possible that I had been wrong about Father Gianni and he had been conspiring against me?

Trying to absorb the possibility of his betrayal, I recollected every detail of my meeting with the priest after I asked him to inquire about Allegra's fate. He said he had written to the present-day Abbess at the convent and was awaiting a response, but did I know that to be true? If it wasn't true, why would he have lied to me? Such a deception would alter the sacredness of his vow as a priest and the promise he made to me as a friend.

My fingers curled around Byron's memoir, clutching it tightly in my lap. I was moving into uncharted territory where I had little to guide me but my own belief that on this journey I would find the answers I sought. The land of truth and newfound hope. So satisfying that the world could still offer such unexpected turns at this stage of my life.

'Aunt Claire?' Paula's familiar voice interrupted my thoughts as she strolled into the room with Georgiana in hand. 'Are you all right?'

Turning to them with a smile of assent, I set my spectacles and the memoir on the tea table. 'Byron's reflections brought back old memories – some of them pleasant, some less so – but I feel more convinced that we can trust Trelawny.'

She frowned. 'I am not totally convinced. His story seemed rather contrived to me, but I will give him a chance, for *your* sake.'

'And that is not a pardon, trust me.'

'What of your visit with Matteo at Le Murate? Did he admit to knowing anything about the theft of your sketch?'

'No.' I patted my lap and Georgiana eagerly settled into her usual spot, immediately reaching up to play with my gold locket. 'But he did say something rather disturbing about Father Gianni.' I added the rest of the details from his insinuations against the priest, watching as Paula's reaction turned from surprise into bewilderment.

'Did you believe Matteo?'

'I hardly know what to think . . . but why would a doomed man lie?' I posed.

Not responding at first, she slid on to the settee and arranged the folds of her blue muslin dress, smoothing down each section slowly and carefully. 'I liked Father Gianni, but I had heard rumors around Florence about his past indiscretions. Of course, that may have been idle chatter, but he did not take the vows of the Church until later in life and much about his early life may have been hushed up. Who can say for certain? But the thought of being misled by people whom we trusted makes me think that we should question everyone's motives.'

'We must not become jaded, Paula – if only for Georgiana's sake. She needs to believe in a world where the light of optimism shines forth. And it will, even if it takes time and effort.' Still, I could not blame Paula for feeling uncertainty at this point. Every person in our lives had hidden some secret from us – except Raphael. 'Aside from Father Gianni's behavior, the theft of the Cades sketch *was* a cruel act, but I have every hope that it will be recovered – truly, I do. We can never give up, my dear.' I leaned my cheek against Georgiana's head.

Paula's eyes softened as she watched the two of us. 'No, we cannot.'

We sat in silence for a few minutes. No matter what occurred yesterday or today, the future still held many possibilities . . . life's shifting kaleidoscope of fate. 'Maybe I should consider visiting Le Murate again this evening—'

'No!' She began to rise in protest, but I motioned her down.

'But Matteo may have been holding back information because of Trelawny's presence. His last words were for me alone, and I believe he would have shared more if he had not been interrupted by Lieutenant Baldini before he had a chance to finish,' I explained. 'If I returned on my own, perhaps he would relate the rest of what he knows, and we might have a chance of retrieving the sketch or at least knowing where to begin to find it. It is perhaps worth a try . . .'

'I do not agree,' she said in a firm tone. 'Raphael said that place is awful.'

Raising my head, I picked over my words carefully as I remembered the prison's damp walls and acrid odor. 'It is not

pleasant by any means, but Matteo may know the identity of
our thief, and we need that Cades sketch – it could make all
the difference between living in genteel poverty and enjoying
some degree of well-being.'

'Even if I agreed, Trelawny and Raphael would never
allow it.'

I bristled. 'May I remind you that I do not need a man's
permission to do anything? My actions are my own business.'

That comment elicited a tiny smile from Paula. 'You will
never change, will you, Aunt Claire?'

'Not in that regard.'

'*Sei arribbiata?*' Georgiana asked me, her small face
puckered in concern.

Hugging her tightly, I responded in English, 'No, I am not
angry, my sweet one. Just teasing your mama because she had
a mistaken notion about me. But I have corrected her in this
matter.'

'*Bene, bene.*' Georgiana snuggled into my arms, contented
once more.

'Leave Trelawny to me,' I added. 'After all these years, I
know how to handle him—'

'Oh, you do?' he said, striding into the room with the kind
of energy that seemed to fill up our little sitting room. 'And
what scheme, may I ask, are you hatching that you need to
"handle" me? I thought I heard you mention Le Murate. Do
not propose returning to the prison, because that is not an
option – there is nothing more for you to learn there.'

'I beg to disagree.'

Raphael appeared behind him, carrying a tray with my china
teapot and remaining cups. 'I thought you might like some
refreshment.'

'Oh, perfect – thank you for being so thoughtful.' Paula
beamed, watching him set the tray on the tea table. He then
seated himself next to her and murmured something in Italian
for her ears only, the murmurings of hidden, shared moments
between lovers. She blushed, then recovered quickly. 'May I
pour, Aunt?'

'Please.' I turned to Trelawny as Georgiana slid off my lap
to join her mother on the settee. 'And if I want to return and

continue my conversation with Matteo, I will certainly do so. I appreciate your assistance, Edward, but I have spent most of my life making my own decisions and do not intend to change at this late stage.' I smiled politely.

'You are as obstinate as ever,' he muttered.

I pretended not to hear as Paula handed me a cup of the dark, strong tea. Taking a sip, I savored the earthy, slightly bitter brew for a few moments before I continued, 'Perhaps if I met with Matteo alone, he might be more forthcoming.'

'I doubt it—'

'That remains to be seen.' My fingers tightened around the thin, delicate teacup.

'No, Signora Claire, I do not think Matteo will be able to speak with you again – ever,' Raphael chimed in, his dark eyes clouding with some unspoken emotion. 'There will no more opportunities to visit him in Le Murate.'

'Again, I will be the judge of that—'

'Matteo is dead,' Trelawny stated flatly. 'He apparently died by his own hand en route to Rome.'

My breath caught in my throat. 'It cannot be true.'

'He took some kind of poison, which caused almost instant death.' Trelawny slowly moved toward the fireplace and stared down at the bare hearth.

'How horrible – and a mortal sin.' I set my cup in the saucer, noting a tremor in my hand. After all that Matteo had done, I knew he deserved scant compassion, but I could not help but feel some stirrings of pity for him. Such a sad end.

'Indeed.' Trelawny continued to stare into the emptiness. 'Perhaps he shall see Dante's lines written above the Gates of Hell: "Eternal, and eternal I endure. All hope abandon, ye who enter here."'

Alarm flitted across Paula's face as she took in the import of his words. Quickly, she rose and grasped her daughter's hand with a firm grip. 'I think it is time that Georgiana took a nap—'

'But I want my tea, Mama,' she protested, tugging on Paula's dress.

'Once you are settled, I shall bring you a cup. Come along.'

Reluctantly, Georgiana allowed Paula to draw her out of the

room, though I heard her pose a question to her mama in Italian: '*Cosa c'è che non va?*'

Paula assured Georgiana that nothing was wrong.

Once they had exited, Trelawny turned to me. 'I apologize for blurting out such harsh sentiments in front of the little one . . . I am not used to being around children since my own brood has long been grown – and my daughter, Laetitia, who lives with me, has no children of her own.'

'Apology accepted,' I said, somewhat distracted at the image of Trelawny as a father. I knew all about his many wives and multitude of offspring, since our correspondence had never ceased over the years, but, like me, he never quite became domesticated and none of the relationships had lasted. He had drifted through life alone most of the time, wandering the globe from one adventure to another – always restless, always seeking a new horizon. Needless to say, that did not make for domestic bliss for any woman.

'Perhaps I was somewhat at fault myself,' I conceded as I stared down at my teacup. 'All I can say is my desire to get to the truth of Matteo's actions has made me . . . impatient.'

'Apology accepted, as well.'

Harmony restored, he strolled over and seated himself in the other wingback chair next to mine. I poured him a cup of tea and, as I handed it to him, we exchanged the lenient glances of old friends . . . a familiar compatibility of shared experiences. 'How did you hear about Matteo's death?'

'Lieutenant Baldini caught Raphael and me on the Ponte Vecchio.' Trelawny's hand dwarfed the cup as he attempted to sip the liquid by threading his index finger through the handle. 'When he gave us the news, he seemed angry that his prisoner had been allowed an opportunity to commit suicide as he was being transported to a larger prison in Rome.'

A tiny shudder passed through me, as if I could hear Matteo laughing at having outwitted his jailors. 'It seems so odd considering the penitence Matteo showed during our meeting at Le Murate. Why add to his sins by committing suicide? It does not make sense.'

'I agree.' Trelawny gave up on his maneuvers with the teacup and simply drained it in one long, deep swallow. 'But we will never know for certain since he cannot answer our questions from his new home . . . in hell.'

Raphael crossed himself and murmured a short prayer for mercy in Italian under his breath.

Trelawny did not join him. 'I will grant that Matteo applied swift justice to his own crimes, although, when all is said and done, a guilty man has few choices in the end. He knew he would probably be executed for killing the priest and just moved up the date by becoming his own executioner.'

'But that verdict was for a judge and jury to decide – not Matteo. Perhaps God will show him some grace.' At that point, we fell silent, each of us lost in our own thoughts. Sadly, the one man who might know what forces conspired against me was now dead, and I was back where I had begun when Mr Rossetti first came to Florence – penurious and with nowhere to turn. 'It feels like the final curtain is about to fall on our Florentine drama.'

'*Finito?*' Raphael echoed my sentiments.

'Maybe not.' Trelawny was stroking his gray beard meditatively. 'Why are we thinking so negatively?'

'What do you mean?' I watched as his eyes began to kindle with focused intent, which always meant trouble. 'Father Gianni is dead. Matteo is dead. And all we have is Byron's Ravenna *confessione* and your memories of a few conversations with him during his last days in Missolonghi. It does not seem like much to go on.'

'A lost cause?' He rose to his feet, pacing quickly back and forth in front of the window like the fluttering of an eagle ready for flight. 'In my experience, a cause is only "lost" in the absence of hope. Who would have thought that Greece would throw off the yoke of Turkish oppression? At the time, it seemed unlikely, but Byron persuaded all of us that it was possible – even in the face of overwhelming odds.'

'Or that *Italia* would unify in the Risorgimento?' Raphael added quickly. 'Few believed it would happen.'

In spite of my melancholy reflections over Matteo's death, I felt a quickening of my heart as I translated silently the word Risorgimento: Rising Again.

'Lieutenant Baldini will continue the investigation to find

the Cades sketch, but why can we not pursue our own inquiries about Allegra?' Trelawny halted his pacing in front of me. 'I propose we travel to Ravenna and visit the convent at Bagnacavallo – that is where it all happened. Surely, there are some records that still exist from those days. At the very least, we can talk with the present-day Abbess about Father Gianni. To my mind, it is the only way that you will know for certain about Allegra's fate . . .'

'*Si.*' Raphael rose and stood next to Trelawny. 'We must take this path and see where it ends.'

Their confidence radiated light into the room, but my misgivings remained. I had already been disappointed too many times. Would this odyssey be yet another aborted effort? Could I stand one more lost dream?

'Claire, you must do this – for Allegra,' Trelawny said as he touched my shoulder. 'Otherwise, you will always be filled with remorse and regret. I know those emotions only too well, and they make for miserable companions in life. If you take this journey, at least you will know that you did everything you could to find your daughter.'

I knew all the practical reasons against such a trip: we would stretch our modest resources even more thinly, the roads would be hot and dusty, and I would find the long travel days tiring. But something in my heart told me to take the risk. I still had time for one last adventure and could solve the great mystery of my life – lay to rest the demons from my past.

Raising my chin, I replied simply, 'I will begin to pack tonight.'

Trelawny smiled. 'And I will make the arrangements for us to depart as soon as possible.'

'Where are we going?' Paula appeared once more, a puzzled expression flitting across her face.

'Ravenna,' Raphael said. 'Come into the kitchen with me, and I will explain everything.'

She slipped her hand in his, allowing him to draw her out of the room.

Once they had exited, Trelawny said quietly, 'Before we go any further with these travel plans, tell me honestly: are you prepared for this journey, Claire? I did not mean to push you into it . . . there is no dishonor in declining.'

'I shall be ready to leave in two days' time.' But first I had to make one very important stop at the Basilica di San Lorenzo, the church where Father Gianni had been stabbed. I needed to attend mass at the church that had meant so much to me . . . and see where he died one more time. Stand in that holy place and remember the man whom I once thought I knew so well. I made a mental note to ask Raphael to arrange for a driver to take me in the morning.

I spent the evening with Paula and Georgiana, choosing the personal items that we needed to take on our trip: day and evening dresses for at least a week, as well as our toiletries and items to keep Georgiana entertained on the road. The hotels on our journey would be basic, due to our modest resources, so we had to bring along most of what we would need for the trip. I did not mind. I loved to travel, even at this stage of my life, and this venture had a much hoped-for outcome: a final reckoning with the past.

Georgiana picked up on our sense of excitement, making it difficult for Paula to calm her enough at bedtime, so I brought her into my room and sang a lullaby that I had sung to Allegra to coax her into sleep: 'Lay you down now, and rest, / May thy slumber be blessed / Lullaby, and good night, / You're your mother's delight . . .' By the fourth stanza, her eyes drooped shut and she drifted off into the sweet repose of the young and innocent.

Tucking the quilt under her chin, I touched her cheek as I whispered the last few lines of the song. There was nothing more beautiful than the angelic stillness of a sleeping child. My dear Georgiana. I was so fortunate to be able to enjoy the presence of a child who was just beginning to discover life. Everything seemed fresh and new through her eyes, and it renewed me to see her wonder and bliss. Of course, she would come to know the great joys and great disappointments that came with the years, but, for now, it was enough to watch her softly rhythmic breathing and savor her innocence.

Smiling, I lay down next to her and closed my eyes.

\* \* \*

After a deep and dreamless sleep, I arose in the early morning, careful not to disturb the household, and dressed quickly to attend morning mass. True to his word, Raphael had our driver standing by as I emerged from our apartment. I would have preferred to walk, but, even at this early hour, the temperature was already climbing.

The young Italian *guidatore* helped me into the carriage with a gentle hand, and we set off through the early morning streets of Florence. I loved this time of day before the crowds descended on the shops and markets in the central part of the city, with only delivery wagons and street cleaners for company. Without the masses of people, I could appreciate the Ponte Vecchio's quiet elegance as we passed its craftsmen setting up their tables of fine gold jewelry, then the classic symmetry of the Uffizi colonnade and magnificence of the Piazza del Duomo's cathedral. I never tired of seeing these Florentine landmarks that had remained through centuries of conflict and natural disasters.

A beauty for the ages.

No less so, my destination: the Basilica di San Lorenzo with its rustic terracotta brick exterior and ornate gilded interior – once the parish church of the Medici family. When we arrived, I took a few moments to gather my strength, suppressing all thoughts of the violent scene that I had witnessed here not long ago. Whatever Father Gianni had actually done, he did not deserve to be murdered in his own basilica.

The driver helped me out of the carriage, and I entered through the massive front door, breathing in the main chapel's cool air. Strolling past the columned arcades, I made my way to the high altar and joined the smattering of parishioners waiting for morning mass – mostly old women wearing black and clutching their rosaries as they murmured novenas. I took my seat near the front and stared up at the gold crucifix decorated with a sculpted figure of Jesus. I began my own prayer for the soul of Father Gianni, hoping that he would find his way to heaven. I fervently wished that with all my heart.

I tried to pray for Matteo, but I could not.

My compassion only went so far.

Just then, a bell rang, and we all stood, crossing ourselves as a middle-aged priest entered. He blessed the congregation and then invited us to take part in the Act of Penitence, followed by singing the *Kyrie*. As I sang, though, the familiar sense of peace did not descend over me as I held my rosary. Trying to invoke a sense of serenity, I imagined the benign image of Father Gianni conducting the mass, his face lit with spirituality as he sang the verses in stirring Latin. He was one of the reasons that I became a Catholic at this late stage of my life: he made me believe in the power of charity and forgiveness.

'*Christe, Dei forma humana particeps, eleison.*'

*God have mercy on us.*

I crossed myself as another image of Father Gianni flashed in my memory – this one of his lying at the foot of the Cosimo de' Medici statue in the old Sacristy. Blood flowed from the stab wound in his chest, dark red against the marble floor. No last rites. No final words. Just a river of death. I could never forget it. And now I could not even grieve without another ghost: the specter of doubt that had been raised by Matteo.

The rest of the mass unfolded, but I could not focus with more than feigned solace.

As the priest processed out, I made a tiny cross on my forehead, realizing that it had been a mistake to come here so soon after Father Gianni's murder. The emotions were too raw, too recent. As I began to rise, a man slipped on to the bench next to me, and I turned to see Lieutenant Baldini.

'*Buongiorno*, Signora Clairmont,' he said quietly. 'I stopped by the Palazzo Cruciato a little while ago, and your niece said you were at morning mass.'

I inclined my head with a smile. 'Perhaps you and I both need to be here.'

'But you came for the spiritual renewal, whereas I am investigating a murder.'

'Do you not follow the religion of your country?' I asked, noting that the parishioners nodded to Baldini as they filed out.

Shrugging, he swung his glance toward the high altar. In the space of silence, his young face took on a more aged aspect, as if the burden of experience weighed him down. 'I believe in justice,' he finally said, 'and whatever must be done in its name – not God's – is my purpose for being on the earth. Does it shock you to hear a police officer commit blasphemy?'

'You do not know me very well to even ask that question,' I replied with a note of irony. 'I am hardly one to make moral judgments.'

'Immorality does not interest me unless it drives a man to commit a crime,' he said, fixating on the crucifix. 'Then I find myself very curious since criminals often have ethics but no conscience.'

'Like Matteo?'

'*Si* – he lived and died by his own code, though a villainous one, to be sure.'

I digested his words, slowly and carefully. 'Do you think Matteo told me the truth at Le Murate when he said he knew nothing about the theft of my Cades sketch?'

'Possibly.'

'But we will never know for certain since he . . . died.' I avoided saying the word 'suicide' in a holy place; it did not seem fitting. 'Perhaps he will find atonement in the next world.'

'A sinner's most fervent wish.' Baldini sounded uninterested in the topic as he shifted his attention back on me. 'Your compatriot, Trelawny, informed me that you were traveling to Ravenna . . .'

'We leave tomorrow for the nearby convent at Bagnacavallo where my daughter once lived – I want to see it before I am too old to travel.' It was the truth, albeit a partial one.

'I see.'

Shifting uncomfortably on the hard, wooden bench, I had the sense he guessed more about our proposed trip than he was revealing. 'Is that permitted?'

'Of course. I asked Trelawny to send word periodically on the road – a mere formality, of course – and I will also apprise you of the investigation.' He gave a slight smile. 'You are the *victim* of a crime, not the criminal.'

So why did I feel so guilty?

'I hope we will have found your stolen drawing by the time you return.'

'If that is the case, I will be most grateful. My niece and I are in a rather impoverished state at present, and the sketch could provide us with some relief.' I paused. 'As you know, I had thought about selling my Byron letters, but I could not bring myself to part with them, so the artwork is my only asset.'

'Most assuredly, I will do my best,' he promised. 'And try not to ruminate about Father Gianni's murder. Matteo has paid for his evil deed.'

'That may be difficult, but I shall try.' I rose and he did the same. '*Grazie*, Lieutenant.'

As I turned to leave, I heard him say, 'Do you remember anything else that Matteo said?'

I shook my head, not looking back.

'*Addio*,' I murmured quickly and exited through the front door before he could ask any further questions. The driver helped me into the carriage and I urged him to set off.

As we pulled away, I saw Baldini standing outside the basilica, hands shoved in his pockets as he watched me, his eyes narrowed in the sunlight.

Tell him the *whole* truth, a tiny voice said from inside.

But I could not stop.

Ravenna awaited.


*Palazzo Guiccioli, Ravenna, Italy*
*December 8, 1820*

*Allegra's Story*

Papa said I had to stay inside the palazzo courtyard.

I spent the morning with the contessa who is teaching me how to play the pianoforte. My fingers are quite small, but I can play the chords well enough. Mostly, I like to sing when she plays because Papa always comes in to listen. He said I have the voice of an angel – like my English mama.

I do not remember her very much now, except that she had dark hair and loving eyes. Papa told me that it is best I do not think of her, but sometimes I cannot help it, especially at night when I lie in my bedroom all alone with only my doll for a companion . . .

On Papa's orders, Tita watched me as I played in the palazzo courtyard, which had turned still and silent because of the snowstorm that had swept through Ravenna. The flowerbeds sat bare and empty. And instead of water, ice dripped from the three-tiered fountain that sat in the center. *Freddo* – so cold.

Tita had brought out my wooden wagon and a rocking horse to keep me busy.

While I played, he told me stories about growing up in Venice with his brothers, when they swam the Grand Canal and enjoyed fistfights with Austrian guards – I love hearing his tales and envied his large family. I wished so much for a brother or sister. The servants' children who came to visit occasionally were my only friends. Mostly, I was on my own.

At least I had Tita when Papa was gone.

Just before teatime, Papa's valet, Fletcher, summoned Tita and me inside. He spoke no Italian, but I could tell from the nervous shift in his eyes that he was anxious. As he helped me remove my blue velvet coat, I saw him hand a paper to Tita and utter something in English that I did not understand.

Tita cursed in Italian.

I stood on tiptoe to see what was on the paper; it was a rough outline of Papa's face with the word *Traditore!* splashed across in red ink – the color of blood.

Was Papa a traitor?

# FOUR

'To see thy sunny fields, my Italy,
Nearer and nearer yet, and dearer still . . .'

*The Prophecy of Dante*, II, 67–68

*En route to Ravenna, Italy*
*July 1873*

After two days of travel, it seemed as if we had descended into Purgatory with each mile.

Unfortunately, the evening before we left Florence, Georgiana had developed a slight cough, so I suggested that, instead of heading north to Ravenna, we take a detour to Bagni di Lucca for her to take the waters. Having lived in Italy for many years, I believed the hot springs, which they called *terme*, could cure almost any ailment. Trelawny sent word to a hotel, the Palazzo Fiori, that we would be stopping there overnight, and we finally left in a drizzling rain. A dreary start. And we could afford only one hired carriage for long-distance travel, so all of us – Raphael, Paula, Trelawny, and I, along with Georgiana – squeezed inside the small, enclosed interior.

After the rain cleared, the heat soared. The dust swirled. And we grew more and more irritable as we jarred along the rough, bumpy roads.

Perhaps the change of plans not been such a good idea.

But Bagni di Lucca held lyrical memories for me as an ancient resort town at the foot of the Apennine Mountains which I had visited in my youth – a place to heal body and soul. Admittedly, those sweet days of bathing in thermal springs and sitting in the hot, steamy grotto may have colored my view of its curative power, but Georgiana needed time to revive her health again.

As I had all those years ago.

Shelley, Mary, and I had stayed there in the summer of 1818 and had bathed in the warm waters many times during those halcyon months. When we first arrived and stayed in the main part of the town, we quickly grew tired of the watchful spying of the English tourists who wanted to see if Byron was with us (he was not), and Shelley moved our household from a hotel to the Casa Bertini – a small brightly colored villa tucked away on a nearby wooded slope.

I could have stayed there forever . . .

Sighing, I glanced out of the carriage window and we headed north from Lucca, the countryside changing from Tuscan hills to steeper ridges of lush chestnut and oak trees. The air grew cooler and its scent held an earthly fragrance of forest pine.

'Are you lost in the past?' Trelawny whispered so not to disturb Paula and Georgiana who dozed, along with Raphael, in the seat across from us.

'We spent only a few months here, but it was a golden time . . . I learned to ride horseback in these woods.' I gestured at the thicket of leafy branches that arched over the road.

'You took to it well, I trust?'

'I fell more times that I can count, but it hardly mattered since I was so happy to be in the beauty of nature.'

'Ah . . . the peace of a rural setting,' he mused. 'Nothing quite matches it.'

'Except the quiet of a carriage with sleeping passengers,' I could not resist adding, with a gentle nod in my niece's direction.

Trelawny followed my glance. 'It is difficult for a child and her parent to be confined so long on the road – especially when the little one is ailing.'

'Indeed, yes.'

'Before they awaken, I need to tell you something, and I want you to remain calm. I believe a man is shadowing us,' he said in a low voice.

A cold chill snaked down my spine. 'Are you certain?'

He took a quick glance out of the window and nodded. 'A rider on a bay-colored horse has been behind us for the last four hours, keeping at the same distance when he could easily overtake our carriage. It seems . . . suspicious. Do you have Shelley's and Byron's letters with you?'

'Yes – in my travel case.'

'Good. Keep them out of sight, just to be safe, since they are so valuable.'

'Should we contact Baldini when we arrive?'

'Let me think about it.' He paused. 'I have nothing definite to tell him – just a soldier's sense of disquiet – but I do not like it.'

My own apprehension grew to match his at this point. As I scanned the blur of foliage that passed outside the carriage window, its beauty seemed altered; each tree might be shielding a bandit, each corner hiding a new menace. Was it possible some villain from Florence trailed our little cortege? Why? We had little to steal now since the Cades sketch was gone. Then again, criminals often seemed to prey on those who felt the pinch of hardship.

I shivered in spite of the heat.

'When we arrive, take Paula and Georgiana to their room, and I will tell Raphael to keep watch. He is a strong and capable young man – loyal, as well.'

'I agree that he has been steadfast beyond all expectations.' My gaze drifted over to them, taking in Paula's fair hair and delicate features in repose, her head on Raphael's shoulder, and his contrasting Romanesque appearance – both so young and beautiful. Georgiana nestled between them in contented sleep, her breathing soft and even. A fierce surge of protective-ness stirred inside of me, engulfing all other emotions. My family. They were the only ones left, and I would make sure that nothing happened to them, no matter what. I may not have fought strongly enough for my daughter years ago, but I would fight for my dear ones now.

'Do not fret, Claire,' he assured me. 'I shall keep them safe.'

I shot him a glance of gratitude. In spite of the rift in our friendship, I preferred to have Trelawny with me more than any other man in this type of situation. He could be ruthless when threatened.

We said no more as the carriage creaked along the winding road that skirted the Serchio River, dotted with quiet hamlets of red-roofed villas perched along the banks.

A young man, carrying a basket on his shoulder, stared at our carriage as we approached Borgo a Mozzano, a tiny village that I remembered well.

'The Devil's Bridge,' I pointed out as we passed the Ponte Della Maddalena with its elegant arches spanning the river.

Trelawny lifted a brow in curiosity.

'It was built in the middle ages by the Countess Matilda of Tuscany, so that she could reach the hot springs, but local legend has it that the devil was asked to help construct it; in return, he was offered the soul of the bridge's first traveler which, fortunately, turned out to be a dog.'

'Poor animal,' he said. 'I can think of at least a dozen men I would have marched across the bridge instead.'

'Only twelve?'

He shrugged. 'There may be even more.'

'Let us hope the devil is not still waiting,' I quipped, watching the young man turn from us and make his way across the bridge as he kept a firm hold on the basket. With my newly sparked caution, I kept a wary eye on him until he disappeared behind a large oak tree.

'What is the real reason you wanted to come to Bagni di Lucca, Claire?'

I paused for a few moments. 'Aside from Georgiana's health, I suppose I needed to feel this chapter of my life had closed before I could go on with our journey to the convent. When I stayed here with Shelley and Mary, I had just surrendered Allegra to live with Byron – a loss I felt so keenly that they brought me here to restore my spirits again. I shall always be grateful to Mary for that. But this was the place where I had to make peace with giving up my daughter, and I needed to see it once more before I could reclaim her.'

It made little sense even to my own ears, but I could explain it in no other way. Feelings often floated above any rational signposts and left us stumbling forward at times . . . but at least there was a destination now.

'I understand.'

And perhaps he did . . . more than I did myself.

'I heard that ancient Romans soldiers came here because the *terme*'s healing properties could cure any infirmities of old age – even Julius Caesar sought out the warm springs. The fantasy of every soldier,' Trelawny commented drily. 'I would settle for an easing of my joints.'

'Ever the skeptic.' I resisted smiling at his irony. 'But you may change your mind once you soak in their warmth . . . Napoleon's sister built a summer house nearby and was reputed to have said the thermal springs were a fountain of youth.'

'And yet she died at forty-three – or so I have heard.'

'It is apparent that you have already made up your mind, so I shall not try to convince you otherwise.'

'On the contrary, I am persuadable – but wary at this point.'

*As am I.*

The *terme* cast its spell on everyone who came here, and I could only hope nothing sinister awaited us. Trelawny and I would be on guard from now on.


Half an hour later, the carriage crossed the Ponte a Serraglio and began the climb up a narrow road, halting in front of the Palazzo Fiori – an inn high above the Lima River valley. With its pale-yellow exterior, shuttered windows, and Doric columns across the front, it looked surprisingly elegant – and, true to its name, it was adorned with wildflowers on every side. Blooms of red and pink popped with bright patches of color. All normal.

'How pretty,' Paula commented as her eyes fluttered open and she caught sight of the scenery. Georgiana still dozed quietly.

'You may thank Trelawny – he found the inn close to where I once stayed.' I reached out and placed the back of my hand against Georgiana's forehead. 'She is not running much of a fever . . . that is a good sign.'

'I think the sleep has helped . . . she has not coughed in some time, so I will settle her in our room and let her continue to nap.' Paula lovingly patted her daughter's back, waiting for Raphael to exit the carriage; then she handed Georgiana to him. 'She is very resilient.'

I smiled. 'Like her mother.'

'Thank you, Aunt Claire – it must be a family trait.'

Trelawny helped us out of the carriage, and we followed

Raphael as he carried Georgiana inside the inn's lobby with its marble floors and high ceiling – a welcome reprieve from the dusty clatter of our long day's journey.

We registered and then each retired to our rooms, mine with a view of the lush green landscape that sloped down the mountainside below. As I threw open the window and took in the sunlight flashing streaks of gold between the trees, I found myself remembering the echo of Mary's voice from years ago: *Claire, you must come with us. Shelley and I are going to bathe in the Bagni Caldo – the warm water will help you embrace life once again.*

And it had – eventually.

I would immerse myself in the waters and simply let my mind drift into a calm, empty space. Sweet nothingness.

*Oh, to have that sensation again.*

In the midst of my recollections, I heard Paula's movements next door as she spoke to Georgiana in a soothing tone to calm her fretful whimpers. I waited until they turned silent, then I quickly changed into a white cotton dress and flat shoes. I fastened my hair loosely in a low, simple chignon.

No stockings, no bonnet, no gloves.

Freedom.

I could never be so casual in Florence but, for now, I wanted to discard all the binding clothing demanded by the social modesty that every woman had to embrace to be 'respectable.' All of my wild ways had been firmly tucked away for so long. In my heart, though, I was still Claire Clairmont – passionate and uninhibited. That inner rebel always lurked inside . . .

Letting myself out of the room, I made my way down the stairs and out of the front entrance with a lightness in my step, though I carefully scanned the area. A few young women were ambling back from the hot springs – their hair damp and their faces flushed as they chattered away in Italian. Nothing amiss. Thus, I quickened my pace, knowing exactly where I would go: a hidden stream that fed into the main pool. Following along the river, the woods grew thicker and the air cooler as I climbed higher. Once I drew near the stream, the walking path narrowed with a dense thicket creeping in on all sides, but I was unafraid. I knew what awaited me – and remembered the way only too well.

As I emerged into the clearing, a fast-moving brook of crystal-blue water unfolded before my eyes with a steady, hushed murmur – a natural paradise that lay deserted in the late afternoon. Eagerly, I moved toward the shore's edge, kicking off my shoes along the way.

Wading into the shallow water, its warmth swirled around my legs, silken and soft. Then I closed my eyes and tilted my face upwards to the light, inhaling the damp, mossy scent. I had dreamed of being back here many times, recalling the drowsy summer days that gave me great delight even in the shadow of giving up my daughter. I knew Byron could provide for her in a way that I never could.

*I sent you my child because I love her too well to keep her . . . you who are powerful and noble and the admiration of the world.*

Those had been my words to him.

It had been a painful decision, but Shelley and Mary had persuaded me that it was best. I never really agreed whole-heartedly, yet I had few options, since Byron had made it clear that even if he divorced his wife, he did not want another spouse. I knew that.

Opening my eyes, I tried to come back to the stillness around me, but the past kept edging around reality.

Images of Shelley rose in my mind – perched on one of the rocks, wearing only his breeches as he watched the puffy clouds drift across the sky and scribbled away on a poem. He would read us fragments of his new verse as Mary and I waded in the water, reciting the melodic lines slowly and carefully as he sought the perfect rhyme.

> I bring fresh showers for the thirsting flowers,
> From the seas and the streams;
> I bear light shade for the leaves when laid
> In their noonday dreams.

He finished writing his poem 'The Cloud' the next year in Leghorn, but this little stream had inspired his creative spark.

On the days when he occupied himself with translating something from Plato, Mary and I would sit on the grassy bank, reading reviews of *Frankenstein* and fantasizing about a time when we would not have to move constantly to outrun creditors.

Our free-spirited lifestyle came with a price that we could rarely afford.

Occasionally, Mary and Shelley's young children, William and Clara, would join us, splashing in the water with childish delight. Much as I loved them, seeing them made me long for my own child . . . so much so that I finally persuaded Byron to let me see Allegra. Shelley and I traveled to Venice to see her – and Mary soon followed with the children.

Our idyll ended too soon, for when Mary traveled by forced stages to join us, Clara fell ill from the sweltering summer heat on the road and died in the lobby of a hotel, awaiting the doctor's arrival.

Mary never forgave me.

I tried to help assuage her grief in every way I could, but a mother's love could consume even every inclination toward forgiveness, as I knew only too well.

*Oh, Mary, if I could only take back my actions, but even this Eden was also a sad place without my child.*

The memories gradually dissolved, and I became aware that the sun had intensified, burning against my skin. Quickly, I waded toward a shaded section where a large oak tree offered some cover under its leafy branches. Easing myself on to one of the rocks, I sat there, listening to the endless trickle of the water as it bubbled up and flowed out of its source deep in the earth.

After a few dreamy moments, a branch snapped – and I started, turning my head toward the sound with a rising sense of misgiving. I scanned the trees but caught sight of no one. Keeping myself very still, I strained my ears to hear if someone might be lurking about, but I detected nothing. Then I chided myself for being foolish. Trelawny's warning earlier had made me overly cautious. No one was out there.

Reaching down, I trailed my fingers along the water's surface, lightly skimming the small ripples.

'You look quite peaceful,' a familiar voice said quietly from behind.

This time, I was not startled because Trelawny's voice seemed almost as soothing as the gently flowing spring. 'I wondered how long it would be before you found me.'

'I suspected you would come here first, despite my warnings.'

'Am I that predictable?'

'Only to one who remembers the many times you described this stream in your letters.' He strolled toward me, still wearing his travel clothes, including the jacket and boots, in spite of the heat. Ever the soldier. Halting near the water's edge, he took a quick survey of our surroundings.

'It holds many . . . fond memories – I could not resist its lure.'

'Shelley always said this was one of his favorite places. I believe he called it a "utopian ideal where nature could restore even the most dejected man."'

'That sounds like him.' I remembered Shelley often taking William with him to his favorite spot to watch the sun set behind the mountains to the west. 'But the stay was not without its share of shadows. I resented that Mary had her children with her when all I wanted was the same mother's bliss that she enjoyed. How can that be wrong?' I did not need to say more; he knew all about the ill-fated trip to Venice. 'I blamed Mary for parting me from Allegra, and she blamed me for Clara's death, so I should not be surprised that she was not always honest with me.'

'I, too, had a falling out with Mary, but she loved you – I know that.'

'And begrudged my presence in her life with Shelley,' I added tersely. 'I was like a fifth wheel to a coach – always useful but needlessly present during the times on smooth roads. And all we did was disappoint each other . . .'

'Perhaps that is why you really wanted to come here: to forgive yourself.'

I twisted my head to look up at him, shading my face with my hand. 'It seems foolish to let the past still haunt me, especially when they are all long dead, but ever since I learned the truth about Allegra's supposed death, it has stirred up such deep feelings that all of the events seem as if they occurred only yesterday – though my images of her have dimmed somewhat over time. I need to know the whole truth and maybe she will be real to me again.'

'Trust me, you shall.' Trelawny assisted me on to the bank, then retrieved my shoes. As I slipped them on, I leaned upon him to steady myself. In spite of my ire at his duplicity, he was the only remaining person from that time who knew what had happened. He had been my friend – and more, if only for a short time.

'Do you think, if Shelley had lived, that he and Mary would have stayed together?' I posed as I straightened and shook out my dress. 'After the years in Italy, always restlessly moving from place to place and losing so many children, her love for Shelley had changed. I saw it in the way she looked at him. Disenchanted. As if they had lost the keys to paradise – and I suppose they had in some ways.'

Trelawny frowned, staring off briefly in the distance. 'I saw Mary a few times after she came back to England, and she seemed content enough with her writing and son Percy. Like all of us, she struggled to survive since Shelley's father gave scant financial help, in spite of Percy being his heir. It is difficult to believe that a man as small-minded and vindictive as Sir Timothy could have produced such a brilliant poet as Shelley. I am sure Mary told you that he refused to meet her, even when she became famous as the author of *Frankenstein*. A petty man to the end.'

'She had related it to me – many times.' And it saddened me since I knew Mary so wanted to be accepted by Shelley's family, if only for Percy's sake. 'I would have thought when Mary and Shelley married after the summer in Geneva that Sir Timothy would have relented in his rigid stance against her, but he could not be moved to compassion even by his own grandson.'

'A heartless man,' Trelawny agreed. 'After he died, Mary, her son Percy, and his wife could finally move to Sussex, to Field Place – Shelley's ancestral home. But she was not well by that time and scarcely enjoyed it . . .'

A swell of sympathy stirred inside at the thought of Mary's last days without me, yet it was mixed with anger. 'She may have been mistreated by her father-in-law but, in truth, it was hardly fair when *she* refused to correspond with me after some perceived slight – and then cut me out of Shelley's biography. I know she spent her later years trying to assume the respectable role of "famous author," but that did not mean she had to rewrite the past – without me.'

'I make no excuses for her, except to say there must have been more at work than we know. She did not treat me kindly either – then again, I was never an easy man to tolerate for very long, as my wives could tell you.' He urged me toward the walking path. 'Come, let us stroll back to the inn before sunset – I do not care for all this open ground when that suspicious rider may be about.'

Nodding quickly, I linked my arm through his and said no more, but my thoughts remained on Mary and our complicated relationship. We had shared every significant event in our lives, both the good and bad, yet she had chosen to separate herself from me late in life. She was my stepsister and my friend – and, later, a jealous rival for the legacy of Shelley's reputation. But he never loved me as more than a dear friend. It was never a competition, except in her own thoughts, for he prized her above all women, and all I ever wanted was Byron. She knew that, but she had driven me away, nonetheless.

Why?

'Do not ruminate so, Claire,' Trelawny urged as he guided me around a towering oak tree. 'It serves no purpose.'

'You are right, of course,' I said, treading carefully over the uneven path where gnarled roots had grown wild. 'I feel as if I can let go of this now.'

'Then the stop in Bagni di Lucca was worth it.'

*I think so . . .*

The path widened and the foliage grew less dense as we drew nearer to the inn, but darkness was closing in and we quickened our pace.

I stumbled over a large root and Trelawny caught me before I fell, urging me along. Moments later, I heard a branch snap, but it seemed closer. 'Did you hear that?' I whispered.

Placing a finger to his mouth, he nodded mutely. We stood in place, waiting . . . as if we had seen lightning and now

expected thunder. But all remained silent. After a few moments,
I exhaled in a long sigh of relief.

*Fuori pericolo* – we were safe.

Then a much louder crack echoed from above and I glanced
upward to see a large, thick tree limb breaking off from the
trunk. Trelawny quickly pulled me away, just before the branch
thudded to the ground, pieces of bark and leaves scattering in
all directions.

Clutching Trelawny tightly, I choked back a cry of fright
– but just barely.

'Stay quiet,' he murmured as he moved toward the tree and
circled around the trunk, kicking at the underbrush as he carved
a path through the low vines and wild shrubs. I lost sight of
him but could hear his thrashing about, muttering curses, as
he crisscrossed through the woods.

Nervously, I curled my hands into tights fists, trying hard
to keep my fragile control intact until he returned. A tense,
wordless anxiety threaded through the air . . . and my thoughts
began to race into shuddering possibilities. Had someone cut
that branch deliberately to fall on us? If so, was the stalker
still lurking in the twilight, looking for another opportunity?
Before panic overtook me, I spied Trelawny's tall figure
moving back in my direction. Eagerly, I reached out to him
and grasped his arm. 'Did you see anyone?'

'No . . . it must have been just a dead limb that fell when
we were passing underneath – nothing else.' He placed a hand
at the small of my back and nudged me forward. 'But aside
from that, there is no point in lingering here since wild animals
come out at dusk and I have no firearm with me.'

Only somewhat relieved, I did not need a second warning
to hurry back to the Palazzo Fiori. The Italian animal world
could be threatening, especially at night, with all types of
creatures. Wild cats. Foxes. Even wild boars. Once we arrived,
Trelawny escorted me to my room, taking his leave until dinner
that evening. He did not seem too alarmed about the incident,
but I could tell that he had not dismissed it either.

I locked the door behind me, lit a gas lamp, and sat on the
bed, staring uneasily at the decorations in my chamber: pretty
silk curtains and lace doilies. A lady's room. And yet somehow

disquieting. I had wanted an adventure, but it appeared that I had, in fact, taken on much more. This journey had taken a distinct turn into the unknown . . . maybe even peril – all stemming from my search to know Allegra's fate and what happened in Ravenna so long ago.

I reached for my spectacles once more.

*Palazzo Guiccioli, Ravenna, Italy*
*December 8, 1820*

*Danger was all around the city.*

*I could breathe it in the streets where people gathered in small groups, murmuring about revolution.*

*The soldier who was shot outside the palazzo last night died in my arms.*

*Tita and I had carried him inside, but I realized that it was pointless to call a doctor. He had taken two bullets to the chest. All we could do was cover him with a blanket and try to make him comfortable.*

*As he lay dying in my study, I learned his name and identity: Luigi dal Pinto – the young Austrian military commandant of Ravenna. My servants grew nervous at his revelation, but I assured them that we were not in danger. Later, I told Tita to remove the rifles to a safe place outside Ravenna and post a watch along the Via Cavour. Luigi's death had been a brutal assassination, and his family would want revenge.*

*Fortunately, Teresa was staying with her father, Count Gamba, at their country estate.*

*I could not say for certain that the Carbonari were respon-sible for the commandant's murder, but I had my suspicions.*

*The first death – on my doorstep.*

*I believed in the necessity of the coming rebellion and yet, as I watched Luigi's last gasp, I felt the weight of his violent end because he was young and scared to die. The sad reality of revolt. It would be first of many, no doubt – I understood that. But I could still mourn that some men had to die for others to be free.*

La rivoluzione.

*By afternoon, the soldiers came to remove his body and they searched the palazzo in grim-faced silence, questioning my servants with careful, pointed queries. They asked few questions of me since I was an English lord and a visitor in their country, but I knew they watched my movements because Teresa's brother and father were known insurgents. And I had seen the posters labeling me a traitor. As the* polizia *inspected the palazzo, room by room, they encountered my mastiff, two cats, a hawk, and my tame crow. Smiling as I overheard them grumble,* molto pazzo, *I realized that my reputation as a mad Englishman worked to my advantage. An eccentric foreign poet could hardly be suspected of plotting with the Carbonari.*

*After they departed, I spent the rest of the day writing letters, then ordered my carriage and instructed Tita to keep Allegra close to him until I returned. I had to see Teresa to know she was safe. He told me that three men had been stabbed in separate incidents around the city only an hour ago – and all of them had died.*

*I vowed to remain alert.*

*Reluctantly, he brought my greatcoat and pistols, urging caution since the public's anger had reached a fever pitch over the murder, and my carriage – a reproduction of Napoleon's – was instantly recognizable.*

*Even my driver, Guido, kept a pistol by his side.*

*As we traveled through the streets of Ravenna in the early evening, it had turned eerily quiet. The snow had melted after a sirocco blew in from the south today, causing the weather to shift into light mist mixed with African red sand – locals called it 'blood rain' and said it was a sign of dark times ahead.*

*Once my carriage exited through the city's* centro, *the tension lifted slightly as we drove through the umbrella pine forest that stretched south to Filetto. I inhaled the pungent, heady scent of the towering trees that reminded me of the thick woods around Newstead Abbey – my ancestral estate in Nottinghamshire. My home. It was barely habitable when I inherited the place, a run-down ruin of its former glory, but I still remembered it fondly and grieved that I would never see it again.*

*I had accepted that fate when I left Venice and had to choose between returning to England or joining Teresa and her family here.*

*I chose Ravenna.*

*As the carriage drew up to Count Gamba's country home – a three-storied Baroque-style villa – Teresa's brother, Pietro, rushed out of the entrance to inform me that the Austrian government meant to strike back after the commandant's murder: the cardinal had issued arrest warrants for any suspected Carbonari involved in the shooting, including Pietro.*

*He admitted to being involved.*

*Then he asked me what could be done if they came tonight to arrest him. I handed him one of my pistols and told him I would ready my turba. 'We must fight – defend ourselves as long as possible. There is no other way now that the die has been cast.'*

*Nodding, he shoved the pistol inside his coat.*

*We made a quick plan for an escape route should we be overrun and then joined Teresa and her father inside. She sat playing at the pianoforte while Count Gamba read a copy of Machiavelli's* The Prince. *A blazing fire warmed the room, casting a golden light around the richly appointed parlor. When I entered, she stopped mid-note and smiled for me alone. The Count greeted me with his usual kind pleasantries, and she kissed both my cheeks in love and affection. It was almost as if they were the family I never had. My own mother had disliked me because of my club foot; my father, 'Mad Jack' Byron, deserted us when I was an infant. I had no one.*

*But now I did.*

*With Teresa present, we did not speak of the commandant's assassination or the murderous aftermath, but I noted that the count's glance flicked between the mantle clock and Pietro, keeping track as the minutes ticked by. When the polizia did not appear, we shared a light supper and the Gambas left me alone with Teresa for an hour while they checked on the horses; she and I made love and promised each other eternal loyalty.*

*At eleven p.m., we heard a loud pounding on the front door, and I reached for my pistol as the Count and Pietro hurried in, both with weapons in hand. Sensing danger, Teresa blew out the candles and we stood in the firelight, ready for what would come. The parlor door slowly creaked open, and one of the servants poked his head in and said in Italian, 'There was no arrest order for Count Pietro – he is safe for the time being.'*

*Teresa gave an exclamation of joy as she embraced her brother. We lit the candles and poured some wine. All was well – at least for now – but the Gambas decided to remain at their country estate outside Ravenna; it was too dangerous to return.*

*I took my leave at midnight.*

*As my carriage moved through the forest on the way back to Ravenna, a damp, hard freeze took hold, turning the road icy and perilous. At one point, when the wheels slipped on an outcropping of stone, Guido asked whether we should turn back, but I told him to journey on – I could not leave Allegra alone with only Tita at the palazzo any longer.*

*Even though I kept the glass window closed tightly, I felt the biting cold of the wind through the thin carriage walls. A frigid chill that seeped into my bones. Hunching deeper into my coat's high collar to stay warm, I felt my club foot begin to ache as the temperature dropped lower.*

*To distract myself, I began to chant an Albanian war song that I had learned on my Grand Tour fresh out of Cambridge. Later, I sang it quite often, especially during that Geneva summer of 1816 – so much so that Shelley and Mary bestowed the moniker* Albe *on me. They still referred to me by that nickname in their letters.* Albe.

*I liked it.*

*Then, the carriage halted, and I opened the window to inquire as to why we had stopped.*

*'My lord, please lower your voice,' Guido urged in a low tone. 'Your song was* molto rumorosa *and could be heard all around. There are government spies everywhere who may be waiting for a chance to strike while you are isolated and alone outside of the city.'*

'Scusi.'

*I closed the window and he moved forward again.*

*As we approached the Porta Adriana gateway where I had*

*first entered Ravenna last Christmas, the clouds cleared and a bright half-moon appeared. A bit of good fortune since the light would make it difficult to hide the Austrians' movements in the city.*

*All at once, a cracking sound pierced the air and something thumped against the side of the carriage. I realized that a bullet had hit the door. Another shot rang out, and Guido tipped over, hitting the ground with a thud. Reaching for my firearm, a bullet shattered the window, and I crouched down.*

*I was under attack.*

# FIVE

'What is there wanting then to set thee free,
And show thy beauty in its fullest light?'

*The Prophecy of Dante*, II, 142–143

*Bagni di Lucca, Italy*
*July 1873*

A loud pounding sound echoed inside my mind, forceful and relentless. It halted, then began once more with even greater insistence. Struggling to awareness, I could not tell if I was hearing my own heartbeat or if it was some unknown knocking outside my own psyche.

*Go away – I want to sleep.*

More hammering.

Groaning, I reluctantly opened my eyes to warm sunlight streaming through the window and across my bed. I had slept through supper and the rest of the evening. Sitting up, I realized that I still wore my spectacles and the white dress from the previous evening. Byron's *confessione* lay at my side. How could I have fallen asleep while reading about his encounter with a would-be assassin in the woods of Filetto? The danger and intrigue had been riveting, but I suppose fatigue from the long journey to Bagni di Lucca had overcome me. I was fully awake now, though. Reaching quickly for the memoir, I flipped through page after page to find the point where I had stopped reading – but was interrupted by the knocking again.

'Aunt Claire! Are you awake?' Paula exclaimed from outside.

'Just a moment, please,' I called out. I skimmed over his writing as I tried to find the passage when he encountered the shooter, but stopped abruptly at the section when he and Teresa shared an interlude at the Villa Gamba. Slamming the memoir shut, I tossed it on to the bed. *Damn him anyway.*

I rose and moved toward the door, taking a few calming breaths before I let Paula in. When I saw her face, drawn tight with worry, I instantly regretted my slow response. 'I am so sorry, my dear. I did not hear your knocking at the door. All I can say is yesterday's travel wore me down more than I knew, and I was still in a deep slumber.' Offering an apologetic smile, I then asked about Georgiana's cold.

'I took her to the *terme* last night, and she is much improved – no lingering fever at all.' Paula's frown lessened. 'Trelawny told us not to disturb you, so we dined early and turned in, but I was growing worried.'

'I shall be down directly.'

'There is no need to hurry. Trelawny said the carriage has a broken wheel, which he is having repaired, and we are not likely to leave until noon. He thought we might visit the grotto with Georgiana in the meantime to let the steam clear the last of the infection from her lungs.'

The Grotto Paolina – named after Napoleon's sister.

I remembered it well.

'Do you think it would help her?' Paula queried.

Nodding, I assured her that it would be a perfect treatment for Georgiana. 'We can walk there since it is in the same resort as the *terme* – just tucked away on its lowest level.'

'Splendid.' She gave me a brief hug and left.

I closed the door and leaned my forehead against the jamb. I had not planned to visit the Grotto Paolina – though I wanted to make peace with this part of my life. Too many emotional connections. It was the cave where Mary and I spent many an afternoon enjoying the hot steam – *and* the place where I saw Mary's daughter, Clara, for the last time before she died of influenza in Venice. The loss of the child always casts a shadow over even the brightest of days – not always visible, but always there, nonetheless.

Then again, perhaps seeing Georgiana in the grotto would bring the focus on to her sweet buoyancy.

A new memory in *this* time and place.

Locals said the Grotto Paolina's heat came from a volcano

that existed underneath the cave, but I never quite believed that explanation. Still, who could say? Certainly, the thought of fire and lava just waiting to erupt made for a good story to attract tourists – and distract me from my own tense situation.

Raising my head, I glanced over at the bed where Byron's memoir lay, gauging whether I had time to read a few more pages about the assassin in the woods. But I knew better. It would have to wait.

I slipped on a fresh cotton dress, completed a hasty *toilette*, and reached the dining room with scant time to spare for more than a few nibbles of bread and a cup of tea before Paula appeared. Georgiana trailed in her wake with slow steps and a sleepy-eyed silence. When she saw me, she perked up and quickened her gait.

She reached for my hand eagerly. 'Mama said we are going somewhere special today.'

Leaning down, I kissed her forehead, happily noting that her temperature seemed normal again. 'Yes . . . a grotto.'

She looked up at me with a puzzled expression as I straightened again.

'It is a very old cave where people have gone for centuries to feel better – you will see, trust me.' I squeezed her fingers. 'It will bring the bloom back into your cheeks, my dear, and a lively spark into your spirits—'

'No! I can barely keep up with her now,' Paula cut in with mock alarm.

Laughing, we drew Georgiana out of the dining room and through the busy lobby toward the front entrance. 'Is Raphael going to join us?' I asked as we emerged into the cool morning air.

'No, he is helping Trelawny.'

'Then we shall enjoy this glorious moment together – just the three of us,' I said, feeling a surge of contentment in the company of the two people I loved most in the world. The shadows already felt as if they were fading as we strolled along the very public pathway – perfectly safe. I answered Georgiana's many questions about the grotto – she was particularly curious about the volcano folk legend – and assured her that it was safe.

Walking under a brick archway, we halted in front of the *terme* resort that had been Paolina Buonaparte's vision – a large, rambling building that stood perched on the side of the mountain above the Val di Lima. With stately, classic lines, the fashionable health spa had been built around the simple structure used during Roman times. No ornate pillars or opulent gilt trim – just clean, elegant angles designed to merge with the beech trees and blackberry bushes that surrounded the grounds.

Once we entered, a young woman greeted us with a smile, showed us where to change into thin chemises, then led us down several levels to the Grotto Paolina. Once we entered the small cave, the hot steam enveloped us with a heavy, moist feel to the air. A smallish space, the cave's walls were not much more than the width of a carriage, with rocky outcroppings jutting in from the sides. But the base had seats carved from stone, and we huddled together, breathing in deeply.

I sat in this very spot almost five decades ago.

Oddly, nothing had really changed.

The grotto had been here for centuries, and although visitors changed with each generation, the cave remained exactly how I remembered it – except that those who had been with me were no longer here. Was that not the irony of human thought? We believed so strongly in our own power, but the earth paid us little heed beyond allowing us a temporary stay. Dictators and dreamers had stopped here, but time was the great equalizer of all ambition, keeping the world turning beyond one man's dream.

> 'My name is Ozymandias, king of kings;
> Look on my works, ye Mighty, and despair!'
> Nothing beside remains.

Shelley had written those lines about the vanity of a pharaoh, and they were no less true today. But as I glanced around the grotto, something of the past still lingered – perhaps only in my own mind, but I could see Mary and her daughter, Clara, as if they were in the very places where Paula and Georgiana now sat. Mother and daughter. Fair-haired and full of love. So dear to me.

'Aunt Claire, is the heat too strong?' Paula asked as she dabbed at Georgiana's face with a towel.

Shaking my head, I pushed the images of those long gone out of my mind and focused on my niece's sweet face. 'Actually, I find it quite comfortable since I have grown more sensitive to the cold from my years in Italy. But being in the grotto has caused some old memories to come back, things that I have not thought of in many years. I suppose some part of me wanted to recall them when I urged Trelawny to stop at Bagni di Lucca, but all the old conflicts and rivalries seem undiminished – and still as painful. No matter how many times I recollect the events, I cannot undo what happened to Mary's daughter. I was partly to blame . . .' My voice trailed off into a whisper. I did not need to say more since I had told Paula many times about Clara's death in Venice.

'You could not have known that Clara would sicken on the trip,' Paula said as she stroked Georgiana's hair. 'Age and wisdom can transform us, but we cannot possess those qualities when young. We have to learn from the lessons of life.'

'Indeed.' I leaned my head back against the stony wall. 'You have become quite philosophical.'

'It must be the steam – it has expanded my lungs *and* my mind.'

I laughed.

'Aunt Claire, whatever occurred, *you* have also suffered – and not just from losing your own daughter, but having to live with regret for so long,' she added. 'Perhaps you wanted to come here to finally release those feelings . . . I think you have done your penance.' She placed a hand against Georgiana's back and felt her breathing. 'And I believe the grotto has cleared the last trace of her congestion.'

'*Molto bene.*' She was right. There was nothing else to be learned here, except that I needed to forgive myself for being young and thoughtless – and know that I was no longer that woman. 'Let us go and cool off.' I took in one last, deep breath and rose slowly as I grasped Georgiana's hand. As our little trio emerged from the grotto, the same young woman who brought us there was waiting with an herbal tisane. As we sipped the tea, she guided us to another room where we bathed in cold water to stimulate our circulation. After we finished and dressed again, I felt refreshed in a way that I had not in years – both in body and spirit.

We then made our way back to the Palazzo Fiori, picking wildflowers that grew alongside the cleared path. The sun had risen almost to mid-sky, and a gentle breeze had swept in from the mountains off to the east. Relaxed and happy, Paula and I watched Georgiana skip out ahead of us with her usual energy. All had turned bright with the world for just this moment. And I had what I needed now for the next stage of our journey – some clarity of the past that would help me accept whatever lay ahead.

Trelawny was waiting for us as we reached the inn, dressed for travel in breeches and jacket, his hair tied back neatly with a thin black ribbon. 'I do not need to ask whether you had an enjoyable morning.' His glance took in the three of us.

'It was most . . . enlightening,' I replied, tucking a small yellow bloom behind Georgiana's ear. 'And cured what ailed us.'

'I am happy to hear that.' He reached down and swung Georgiana high in his arms, looking her over carefully as she giggled in excitement. 'This little one looks to be in capital health once again, so we should be able to leave—'

'The wheel is mended, then?' Paula asked.

'Like new.' Trelawny set Georgiana down again, ruffling her hair. 'We can be ready to depart within the hour if you like. Raphael is waiting inside to assist you with the luggage, and I have sent word to an inn near Bologna that we will be stopping overnight – we should then reach Bagnacavello within another day. I also sent a note to Baldini as to our travel plans.'

He'd contacted Baldini. That meant Trelawny thought we might be in jeopardy.

My happy moment faded as quickly as it had appeared. 'Thank you for making the arrangements, Edward.'

'My pleasure.'

Paula also extended her appreciation, then drew Georgiana toward the inn.

As we watched them disappear inside, I turned to Trelawny. 'What about the rider whom you suspected of following us? Do you think he may reappear?'

'I cannot say for certain, but I am taking no chances,' he said in a low voice. 'In truth, that wheel was not broken. Raphael and I spent the morning hiring a horse, so I can ride alongside the carriage. That way, if the mystery rider shows up again, I can move quickly to find his intent while Raphael protects you from the inside.'

A warning voice flared in my thoughts. 'Did you tell Baldini when you sent him the note?'

'Not yet. I decided to wait until I had concrete evidence, but we must remain vigilant.'

The voice grew louder, and I glanced nervously over my shoulder at the thicket of trees just behind us. There were many such places along the road to Bagnacavallo where a brigand could hide, just waiting for the moment to attack our cortege.

'Do not worry, Claire,' he said, covering my hand with a reassuring clasp. 'We are taking well-traveled routes and are expected at reserved inns along the way, so we shall be quite secure.' He linked my arm through his. 'So, what was so "enlightening" about your morning?'

I paused, struggling to allay my fears. 'I laid a few more demons to rest – ones that have haunted me for a lifetime. As a Catholic, I have used the word "forgiveness," but I do not think I truly understood that my own actions could also be absolved—'

'And mine, as well?'

Glancing briefly at his weathered face, I tried to summon a sense of similar charity toward him, but it would not come. 'I understand that you had good intentions – or at least you thought to honor your vow to Byron – but it is still difficult for me to accept that you deceived me year after year. It was not the action of a careless youth. You made a deliberate choice when you knew how much it pained me to have lost Allegra.' Casting my eyes down for a moment, I sighed. 'I am trying . . .'

'I can ask no more for now.' As he ushered me toward the Palazzo Fiori's entrance, he changed the subject and outlined our upcoming journey east to Bologna, then on to Bagnacavallo. It would be an arduous day, then one more after that, but the roads were decent, and I was used to travel in Italy. The destination would more than make up for the long trip.

Just then, a driver brought the carriage up and Raphael emerged from the interior. He held open the door with a large smile. 'Everything is arranged for our departure – we can leave within the hour if you like.'

'Indeed, yes. I am most anxious to arrive at the next stage of our journey.' With a quick nod at them, I hurried toward my room to make ready. I changed into my travel dress and cape, freshened up, and had my trunk taken downstairs, having packed Shelley's and Byron's letters – but not the memoir. Holding it tightly, I took one last glance around the room and realized that it was unlikely that I would ever return. No matter what lay ahead, this chapter of my life was closed. And with it, the recollections of Mary and Shelley, young and laughing in the Bagni Caldi as they dreamed of a future that would be bold and bright, passed away into the realm of days gone by – over and finished.

I let myself out of the room and closed the door firmly behind me.

Later, several hours into our trip, I found myself somewhat more relaxed, knowing Trelawny rode at our side. Also, unlike the previous stage filled with fretful irritation, we passed the time in quiet content while Georgiana read a Ruskin fairy tale, and Paula occupied herself with embroidering a pillowcase. After only a few miles, Raphael had grown bored and was sitting outside next to the driver. I could hear snatches of their conversation in Italian, appreciating the beauty of their Florentine accent as they discussed politics and pasta. If every day passed similarly, the journey to Bagnacavallo would be quite pleasant.

'Aunt Claire, may I ask you something?' Paula said, intent on her needlework, weaving jewel-toned threads into her piece of muslin.

'Of course.'

'Why did you and Trelawny never marry?'

I laughed.

'Now that I have met him and seen your regard for each

other, I am curious why you never chose to make a life with him.' She looked up, pausing mid-stitch. 'He is a fine figure of a man, even at his age, and you have a shared history, to say the least.'

Still amused, I responded with a shrug. 'He asked me many times, but I could never find it in myself to accept.'

'Was it because you always loved Byron?'

'Partly, I suppose.' Hearing his name caused that familiar tug at my heart. Byron. Always and forever. 'How could I ever look at another man, except in contrast to him? That all-consuming love never totally went away, even when I was furious with him about Allegra.'

She studied me for a few moments. 'I cannot imagine what it was like to have loved in that way. I cared deeply for Georgiana's father, and I truly love Raphael with all my heart, but I would never risk everything for love of them—'

'That is because you have Georgiana – *she* is your life,' I interjected with a quick glance at my great-niece, head bent over her book and lips murmuring the words under her breath. 'I would have probably felt the same if I had kept Allegra with me.'

'Perhaps.' She resumed her embroidery. 'But that still does not fully explain your rejection of Trelawny.'

Glancing out of the open window, I watched as the land-scape shifted from rolling hills and cypress trees into the Apennine forest, thick with towering pines. The air grew cooler and the road bumpy as we moved higher into the mountains. 'I suppose it never seemed the right time. We began as friends in Pisa. Then, after Shelley died and Byron left for Cephalonia, our little circle scattered to the winds. Trelawny stayed on to fight in Greece, and I went to Russia – then Germany, Italy, and England. Then back to Florence a few years ago. I never could settle anywhere for too long. It was the same for Trelawny. He traveled the world, picking up three wives along the way – then leaving them behind when he moved on.'

She raised a brow. 'As I said, you are very much alike in many ways.'

'Maybe too much so,' I said drily as Trelawny rode alongside my window, tall and straight in the saddle from a lifetime of being on horseback. He stared off intently into the distance and then moved forward at a faster pace ahead of the carriage. My friend – and lover. 'I never told you this, but Trelawny and I spent a night together. It was in 1822. Shelley had recently drowned at sea, and Mary had left for England with her son. I was alone at the house on the Arno . . . It was a beautiful autumn night and we turned to each other in our grief and loneliness.' And maybe something more . . .

She did not seem surprised. 'But you could have remained together. Nothing stood in your way.'

Except Byron – the man I loved more than life itself. And Mary – the woman who had long been the object of Trelawny's fascination. I vividly remembered parts of what I had written in my journal three years after my interlude with Trelawny:

> I think a great deal of past times today . . . but the sentiments of that time are most likely long ago vanished into air. This is life. So live to nothing but toil and trouble – all its sweets are like the day whose anniversary this is – more transitory than a shade – yet had it been otherwise, if Trelawny had been different, I might have been as happy as I am wretched . . .

But he was not different, as he had shown me by asking Mary to wed him and, later, moving on to other women . . . not to mention deceiving me about Allegra.

'Did you not want any more children?'

'No.' I held my handkerchief to my face to block out the dust kicked up by Trelawny's horse. 'Losing one child was almost more than I could bear . . . I could not endure that kind of pain again. Even though Trelawny lost three of his seven children, it is different for a man, I think.'

'It seems so.' Her face turned pensive as she set her needlework down. 'Georgiana's father has little interest in her beyond sending us a pittance – and she is such a sweet girl.'

I patted her hand. 'But Raphael loves her dearly—'

'Yes, of course. That is more than I had hoped for when Georgiana and I came to Florence to live with you.'

'*La fortuna* – it has turned your way in this regard.'

She picked up her embroidery. 'Does Trelawny even have a chance to win your affections?'

'After everything that has happened?' I shook my head. 'I trust him to see us through this journey, but that is all.'

'Feelings can change . . .'

'Not in this instance – I do not want to love again.'

She did not respond at first. 'It may seem that way now, as I know only too well. When Georgiana's father left us without money or resources, I swore that I would never allow my heart to be broken again. But the anger and bitterness faded – and then I met Raphael and found myself won over by his steady devotion.' Paula reached for her sewing bag and sorted around the contents, bringing out a bright yellow skein of cotton thread. She then threaded the needle with swift, sure motions and began adding tiny new stitches into the fabric. 'It may be the same for you.'

'I think not.'

Although Paula kept her head down, I sensed she was hiding her response. Perhaps my emotions were not as firm as I let on, but I could hardly speak of new beginnings when so much still lay unknown about our adventure's end. 'I shall always be grateful that he chose to reveal the truth, even at this late stage, and is trying to make amends with his usual military precision. He was always the person who could be counted on to handle every aspect of an unexpected turn of fate – no matter how harsh or overwhelming. That is his strength.'

At that moment, the carriage rolled over a large bump in the road, causing us to lurch to one side. Paula cried out as she pricked her finger with the needle as Georgiana and I righted ourselves in our seats. I gave Paula my handkerchief, and she wound it around her index finger, holding it in place for a few moments.

'You mean after Shelley died?' she asked. 'It must have been such a shock to learn of his death at sea.'

'It was . . . devastating.' Shifting my glance toward the window, I found myself forming the words about the tragedy with a matter-of-fact tone that bespoke the passage of time between then and now. 'We knew something had happened to him – and our friend, Edward Williams. For some reason, they had decided to set sail on the *Don Juan* in the middle of a squall near Leghorn. I do not know why. We waited for days to learn of their fate and then heard the boat had gone down in the Bay of Spezia. Still, we had a dim hope that they may have survived – until Trelawny came to tell us the bodies had washed ashore near Viareggio. We were stunned . . . numb with grief, but he arranged everything – had them buried on the shore, rented a new apartment for us in Pisa, and escorted us there. We had no one. But he took care of the unrelenting details that accompany an untimely demise. The paperwork. The officials. All of it.' I let out a shaky breath. 'He could not have been more helpful.'

'I can only imagine,' she observed. 'He certainly showed a great deal of sensitivity to Mary and you. In many ways, a true friend.'

'I suppose so.' Taking Paula's hand, I carefully unwound the handkerchief and checked her finger. The bleeding had stopped. 'Then again, if he had not taught Shelley how to sail the *Don Juan*, Shelley would not have taken the boat into the rough seas . . .'

She shook her head with firm conviction. 'Trelawny could not have known that Shelley would be so foolhardy – that is hardly his fault.'

'Not by intention, but by his presence,' I said, catching a glimpse of him again as he allowed his horse to fall back, slightly behind the carriage. 'A brilliant poet was never meant to be a warrior.'

'Do you speak of Shelley or Byron?'

'Both, I think.' I crumpled the handkerchief in my hand, then shoved it into my bag next to Byron's memoir. 'And Raphael, as well. We must not let him get too carried away as they once did. He has already risked his life once for us and agreed to take this journey for your sake. Raphael deserves to have a long life ahead of him – shared with you and Georgiana.'

'Do not worry – he is not one to behave rashly. The trials of being orphaned when he was a boy have stripped him of any illusions that he is above being harmed. He knows that life is precarious.' Paula slipped her arm through mine and leaned her head against my shoulder.

'As do we all.' I fastened my glance on Georgiana who had fallen asleep, her book still open on her lap.

I would not lose her.

*La fortuna* was with us now.

Two more hours passed before the carriage stopped at the edge of Vergato, a mountain town about forty kilometers west of Bologna. I spied a garden cafe with tables set beneath a sloping roof covered with thick jasmine vines. Sweet, delicate flowers in the summer sun. As Trelawny helped me out of the carriage, I inhaled the fragrant blooms and they revived me after the long hours on the road.

'But this is quite enchanting,' Paula said, emerging from behind me with a still-sleepy Georgiana in hand. 'How did you find this town, Trelawny?'

He smiled. 'I have crisscrossed *Italia* many times.'

'Whereas I have come this way only once when I traveled here with my *nonna*,' Raphael said as he jumped down from his perch near the carriage driver and pointed at a large Gothic structure with turrets and onion-shaped domes nestled high on a peak. 'But I remember seeing the Rocchetta Mattei as a boy and running through its courtyard and towers.'

She raised a hand to her forehead to shield the sun from her eyes. 'Is it a medieval castle?'

'If only.' Trelawny laughed as he gave instructions to the driver to return in two hours. 'Count Cesare Mattei, an eccentric doctor, lives there along with an entire community of medical charlatans. He built it twenty years ago on the remains of old ruins as the center of his medical "inventions" that are supposed to cure all diseases. They say he is quite mad.'

Intrigued, I followed Paula's glance and noted the odd blend of Moorish and European architectural styles. 'It looks almost like the castles that I saw in Germany – dreamy and fairytale-like, nestled in the trees. If we had time, I should like to speak with him since I learned much about herbs when I lived as a governess in Russia. Many people lived over a century there by consuming only plants.'

'I cannot imagine anything more appalling than to live such

an insufferably long existence,' Trelawny quipped. 'Everyone would be heartily bored at hearing the same stories year after year – the elderly can be so tedious.'

'You speak from experience, I suppose?' Still gazing at the castle, I contemplated the daunting prospect of a life that extended into the next century, seeing Georgiana grow to a young lady and perhaps have children of her own. *Not all bad . . .*

Trelawny offered me his arm. 'Indeed, I do.'

I laughed as he led our little band of travelers to the outdoor tables and summoned the owner. A paunchy, middle-aged man brought out wine for the adults and lemonade for Georgiana; he then served the local specialties himself – cheese, prosciutto, and fresh, fragrant honey dripping from a small, square comb set over a bowl. While Trelawny conversed with him in broken Italian, I found myself drifting into that lulled space of a journey half finished – I did not dare let my thoughts move in the direction of the possible risks on the road or what awaited us at Bagnacavallo. For the latter, at least, it was too tempting to imagine the outcome that I most fervently wished with all my heart.

Allegra – alive and well.

*Oh, my dear child. I would gladly give my heart and soul to see you one more time.*

I touched one of the jasmine blooms that draped around the trellis.

How odd that, in all the intervening seasons since our parting, the wind still whispered its sweet promise of spring, and the sun rose and set with autumnal mellowness – in a steady ebb and flow of the natural world. I marveled that it could still be so beautiful without the presence of my daughter.

'Aunt Claire?' Paula was tapping my arm gently. 'Are you too tired to travel on?'

'Not at all,' I responded, plucking the flower from its vine. 'I was simply appreciating this delightful jasmine.'

Not long afterwards, the owner served us, and we enjoyed our lunch – until Georgiana grew restless and was given permission by her mama to wander in the field of wild poppies nearby. I kept a watchful eye on her. As we finished the last of the wine, Paula asked Raphael to join her on a walk, and they took Georgiana with them, strolling slowly along a gravel path that threaded through the tall grass.

As I watched the three of them depart, I leaned back in my chair contentedly. 'This was a pleasant interlude . . . it makes me almost not want to leave.'

'*Almost.* We must move on if we are to arrive in Bologna before evening.' Trelawny rose to his feet and scanned the field as well as the woods that lay beyond. 'The road to the east has a steep decline after we leave Vergato, winding down the mountain with several sharp curves. I would not attempt it at night, especially with the prospect of that shadow rider.'

Reluctantly, I pushed myself into a standing position. 'You are right . . . it is best not to linger.'

While he settled the bill, I ambled in the same direction as Paula and Raphael, feeling the late-afternoon sunlight filter through my dress with a soft warmth that seeped into my skin. Vergato had a golden quality. Isolated and serene. The kind of place that offered the traveler a restful stillness between mountains and hills – before the final descent into cities that lay below, with their crowded streets and bustling energy. And the truth of what had been hidden from me.

Would I embrace the knowledge?

So much had happened during the last two weeks or so that I was not certain of anything at this point; I only knew that I could not turn back.

The road ahead moved in one direction: the future.

As if on cue, I spied a dark-brown bird descending from on high; a *rondone* – a swift – skimmed along the poppy field, its scythe-like wings floating on the air. Then it gave a piercing call and flew upwards once again in a graceful arc. I had become used to seeing the swifts crowding the Tuscan skies in Florence during the summer, living most of their lives – eating, breathing and sleeping – on their wings, and I envied their freedom. But now I, too, could feel the currents of change draw me away from the known and familiar.

The temptation to linger dissolved as I watched the swift join its flock and head east, lifting ever higher until the birds appeared to be only brown dots in the distant skies . . . and then vanished.

We would follow shortly.

Turning away, I moved toward Trelawny with a new eagerness to my steps. 'If you see to the carriage, I will gather the rest of our party.'

'We are here,' Paula said as she approached with Raphael, hand in hand. Her flushed cheeks and happy smile suggested they had been occupied with more than observing the beauties of nature. Ah, young love . . .

'And Georgiana?' I inquired.

Paula halted, her smile fading as she quickly looked around. 'She ran ahead of us on the path, saying she wanted to pick some wildflowers for you. We were but seconds behind.' A touch of alarm threaded through her voice as she called out Georgiana's name several times.

No response.

'She may have circled around the café . . .' I began uneasily. 'Or gone deeper into the woods.'

'I shall search the grounds,' Trelawny said, striding toward the café.

'And I will backtrack down the path.' Raphael gave Paula a brief embrace and then added, 'Do not fear, my love. She could not have gone far.'

Paula clutched his hand. 'Find her – *please.*'

He kissed her hand before releasing it. Then he hurried into the thicket of trees, knocking branches out of his way and cursing in Italian.

Biting her lip, Paula swung her gaze toward me, her blue eyes clouded with fear. 'I never lost sight of her until just a few minutes ago. How could I have allowed this to occur? My own child . . . I could not live if something happened to her.'

'Do not think like that,' I said in a firm voice as I patted her arm. But, inside, I heard myself say, *Yes, you could, but your heart will never be whole again – as I know only too well.* 'We must not panic because there is no reason to believe she is in danger. They will find her shortly. Truly, I believe that with every fiber of my being.'

She gave a short nod, then hugged me tightly.

'Let us walk toward the poppy field – it will calm you.'

We paced along slowly, and, in a soothing tone, I reminded her that Georgiana never strayed too far from us – ever. 'She will come as soon as she hears Raphael call out her name – trust me.'

'I hope so,' she said, gripping my arm. 'This area is unfamiliar to her, so she could lose her way quite easily – or fall down a hill. Either one is too terrible to contemplate.'

'Courage, my dear.'

We edged along the tall grass, then walked back toward the café. We reached it at the moment Trelawny appeared once again, but when I leveled an inquiring glance his way, he simply shook his head.

Paula's hand went to her mouth to stifle a cry.

'No trace of Georgiana – I am sorry. Come, you need to sit down.' His features grew tight with concern as he escorted her to one of the outdoor chairs. 'Do not fear; Raphael knows these woods fairly well from his trip here as a boy, and can move very quickly through the underbrush – much faster than I. There is no one better equipped to locate her.'

She gave him a grateful half-smile, then slumped forward as she drew in a shaky breath.

Knowing the deep emotions that undoubtedly were churning inside of her, I simply stayed close and watched the forest edge for any sight of Raphael. The long minutes passed in silence . . . endless spaces when even prayer seemed to elude me. All I could do was keep my mind fixated on the here and now. And wait. As I had done many times in my life, not knowing the outcome, but never believing all was lost until the very end.

The cafe owner brought out glasses of water for Paula and me, but Paula waved hers away. I did the same, though I thanked him for his kindness.

Paula began to drum her fingers on the tabletop with a nervous staccato, staring into empty space.

More time passed, and I felt my spirits sink lower. *My dear, sweet Georgiana. Please let her come back to us.* But twilight would set in soon, making her recovery even more difficult . . .

Just then, I heard a tiny giggle.

Instantly, I scanned the trees and spied Raphael striding out of the woods as he carried Georgiana high in his arms. Relief flooded through me. Paula rose quickly and ran over to them, embracing her daughter with a mixture of laughter and tears.

'Thank God,' I heard Trelawny murmur.

I closed my eyes briefly. *The light had been restored to our lives.*

Trelawny and I joined them, each of us clasping Georgiana tightly, then making her promise to never wander off again.

'But I wanted to pick wildflowers for you, Aunt Claire,' she protested, holding up a handful of pink and yellow blooms. 'They are so pretty.'

Taking them from her, Paula added, 'I know, but you should not have left the path without one of us.'

Georgiana's face drooped.

Seeing her crestfallen features, I leaned down and kissed her cheek. 'Everyone appreciates your thoughtfulness, Georgiana, but there are wild animals in the forest, and they can bring harm to a lone little girl.'

'*Si.*' She kicked a stone with her shoe, showing the Clairmont stubbornness even as she agreed.

'*Prego.*' I straightened again and looked to the west; the sun had dipped lower in the sky. 'Let us speak no more of this, since we need to journey on to Bologna before it grows dark.'

Trelawny scanned the horizon as well. 'The carriage will arrive soon – and I asked the café's owner to send for my horse.'

'Excellent.' I reached for Georgiana's hand, but she refused my offer.

'I was *not* alone.' She folded her tiny arms across her chest with a mulish expression. 'A kindly man came by on a big brown horse and showed me the way back here.'

A warning chill swept over me. 'Who was he? Did you recognize him?'

'No – he sat too high in the saddle for me to see him.' She gazed up. 'And he wore a hat that hid most of his face.'

I felt Trelawny stiffen beside me.

Raphael frowned. 'But I saw no one.'

Paula gave an exclamation of impatience. 'You are making

this up, Georgiana, and I am growing quite cross with your antics. Raphael and I will take you inside the café where you are not to leave my sight until we depart.'

'But, Mama—'

'*Silenzio.*' Paula hurried her away with Raphael in tow.

Once they were out of earshot, I confronted Trelawny. 'I am trying to remain calm, but the thought of someone harming Georgiana frightens me terribly. Do you think it was the rider you spotted on the road to Bagni di Lucca?'

'Possibly. If so, we must be very careful in case he is still shadowing us.'

'This is maddening. What could he be after?' I spread my arms wide in helpless confusion.

'Money . . . the Byron letters . . . who knows?' He gestured in Paula's direction. 'Let us keep our suspicions to ourselves for now, since it will only upset your niece even more. Please, stay with them until I return – we will be underway for Bologna shortly.'

For once, I did not argue with him.

Our adventure seemed increasingly on the brink of calamity, and I was having a difficult time controlling my emotions.

After striving to compose myself, I took refuge inside with Paula and Raphael. While they lectured Georgiana, I tried to appear normal and pass the time by reading Byron's *confessione* from the point where I last stopped.

Slipping it out of my bag, it did not take long for me to be caught up in the ambush outside Ravenna . . .

*The Woods of Filetto, Italy*
*December 9, 1820*

*I was going to die.*

*Crouching low in my carriage, I held the loaded pistols next to my chest – ready, should I have to fight.*

*I did not dare to open the carriage door to see where Guido had fallen after he took a bullet. After cracking open the window, I could hear his breathing, so I knew he was still alive – but he would not able to help should the assassin come at me in a rush.*

*Another crack rang out from the shadowy forest, but the bullet missed the carriage. I heard it whistle through the trees behind us.*

*Then silence.*

*He was reloading.*

*I realized that I had to move quickly or Guido could perish from his wound.*

*Reaching for the door handle, I cocked one pistol, tucked the other one in my jacket pocket and heaved myself out of the carriage, landing on the gravel road with my good foot. I straightened, raising my pistol in the direction from where I thought the shots had come and fired. Then I tossed it aside and pulled out the second pistol, holding it high. I would face death the way I had always wanted to – on my feet without fear.*

*I waited to fire again until I could target the assassin and thought I caught sight of di Breme's servant. Stefano? Had he remained in the area after his master had died? Why?*

*The forest turned deadly quiet.*

*Strangely, I did not see my life flash before my mind's eye as so many who faced their final moments. I thought only of my daughter, Allegra – and that I would never see her again in this life.*

*My child of love.*

*She would be the last image I had on this earth . . .*

*Then I heard a faint rustling of tree branches and I turned, aiming the gun in its direction.*

*'Do not shoot!' a man's voice shouted in a ragged tone, as if he had been sprinting a good way.*

*It sounded like Pietro Gamba, but I could not say for certain.*

*Not wavering in my stance, I called out to him for the password that the Carbonari used to identify its members. When he did not respond, I cocked the gun.*

*'D . . . Dante Alighieri,' he stammered. Then he emerged from the shadows, and I exhaled in relief at the sight of Pietro's familiar face. He stumbled forward and wheezed in an effort*

to catch his breath, leaning one arm against his thigh as he bent over.

'You followed us?' I released the hammer and lowered my pistol.

'Si.' He took in a few more breaths before he straightened again. 'I came by horse through the forest path. After you left, Teresa had a premonition that something would happen to you and urged me to follow. I took a shortcut and was not far behind when I heard the shots. My horse bucked and threw me – then I ran. By the time I arrived, whoever shot at you had scuttled away – il codardo.'

'A coward indeed, and I may have recognized him – a spy who worked for di Breme.' Before I could explain, the driver groaned, and I glanced back at him lying on the ground, the red stain beneath his left shoulder. He needed a doctor immediately. 'I will fill you in later – we cannot linger.'

'I will drive the carriage – my horse will find his way home.' Pietro helped me lift Guido into the carriage. Semi-conscious, he moaned in pain as we slid him on to the cushioned seat and I bound the shoulder wound.

Pietro climbed on to the driver's perch as I stayed inside the carriage – and, for the second time in two days, I held a bleeding man in my arms, not sure if he would live or die.

It took only a quarter of an hour to reach the Palazzo Guiccioli. Once we arrived, I immediately dispatched Tita for the doctor and settled Guido in my study without disturbing the servants. They were already on edge.

Pietro and I checked Guido's wound again by candlelight. Though still bleeding, it did not appear to be as bad as the commandant's injuries; the bullet seemed to have exited Guido's shoulder. He kept drifting in and out of consciousness.

'If he dies, we must smuggle the body out of here.' Pietro stared down at the wounded man. 'You cannot be involved in another shooting death at the palazzo; the Austrians are looking for any excuse to arrest you—'

'I had nothing to do with it.'

'But the assassin was aiming for you, and they suspect you are a member of the Carbonari. They will blame you.'

I recalled the poster that had suddenly appeared all over

*Ravenna – with my image and the word* Traditore! *I had dismissed it initially but, after tonight, I realized that I must proceed with caution while Allegra resided with me. As the situation in Ravenna was growing increasingly more volatile, the danger around her also grew. I could risk my own life, but not hers.*

*The time might have arrived for me to make other arrangements for my daughter to keep her out of harm's way. Teresa had mentioned a convent in Bagnacavallo . . .*

*Not long afterwards, Tita appeared with the doctor who cleaned and dressed the wound, declaring that Guido would survive. He then gave him a large dose of laudanum and recommended that we not move him for at least twenty-four hours.*

*After he departed, Pietro and Tita soon followed, and I remained in my study – ever watchful in the night while the wounded man remained in a deep, opium-induced sleep.*

*A hushed silence descended on the palazzo, but outside its walls something wild and powerful was stirring – the call to arms for every man who dreamed of freedom. It would soon overtake us and envelop the country in conflict.*

*There was no stopping it now.*

*Pacing back and forth to the window, I scanned the Via Cavour several times, but saw no one lurking below. Still, I could not quiet my agitated nerves. These minor skirmishes were creating a tension that stretched across the city like a tightening noose. I longed for open war – yet feared it would never come.*

*Like Dante, I wanted to see Italy step out of the abyss of tyranny and find a new way.*

*Let it be soon.*

*My glance fell upon the lines from* The Prophecy of Dante *that I had composed yesterday. I picked up the parchment and read aloud:*

*The storms yet sleep, the clouds still keep their station,*
*The unborn Earthquake yet is in the womb,*
*The bloody Chaos yet expects Creation,*
*But all things are disposing for thy doom . . .*

*I was ready for whatever awaited me.*

*As I set the manuscript sheet on my desk, I heard muffled gunshots away in the distance, and I moved back to the window.*

*A far-off cry pierced the darkness below . . . then nothing.*

*It promised to be a long night.*

# SIX

'But few shall soar upon that eagle's wing,
And look in the sun's face, with eagle's gaze,
All free and fearless . . .'

*The Prophecy of Dante*, III, 70–72

*Vergato, Italy (en route to Bagnacavallo)*
*July 1873*

A tap on my shoulder startled me.
I glanced up to see Trelawny, though my mind was still in the world of pre-revolution Ravenna. Assassins in the dark. Secret societies. Lies and betrayals. A time of such dangerous uncertainty. As I refocused my attention on the present, I noted everyone else in our little cortege had already left the café. Fumbling to remove my spectacles, they slipped from my hands and fell on the floor. He retrieved them, murmuring that we were ready to leave Vergato.

'It should be an uneventful trip,' Trelawny continued, 'now that Georgiana has been suitably chastised.'

'I pray that it is so.' After slipping the Ravenna memoir into my bag, I extended a hand to Trelawny.

'We should still arrive in Bologna before dusk,' he said, escorting me to the carriage, where Raphael already sat next to the driver; Paula and Georgiana were inside, positioned on opposite sides with the glass windows shut tightly. I took my place with them and found neither inclined to talk after the trauma of Georgiana's disappearance. Secure in the knowledge that Trelawny rode near the carriage, I decided perhaps it was best to simply soak in the woodland scenery while our emotions had time to recover.

Once we set out for Bologna along a narrow road, our

journey went rather quickly as we descended to the Po Plain
at the foot of the Apennine Mountains and arrived at the
outskirts of the city in fewer than two hours. We trooped into
the hotel and took to our rooms for an early night. I turned
in almost immediately, too tired to pick up my reading where
I had stopped. Drifting off, though, I found my thoughts drawn
back to the tense moments Byron had described at the Palazzo
Guiccioli, when he anxiously awaited the dawn in the company
of his wounded driver.

The stakes of his gamble with the Carbonari were high: life
and death.

That night I dreamed of the fateful summer of 1816 in
Geneva. The sun had broken through a thick layer of clouds,
and the air smelled fresh. I was strolling happily up the short
path between the Maison Chapuis, where I stayed with the
Shelleys, and Byron's much grander Villa Diodati. Suddenly,
I could not find my way and began to stumble blindly through
the underbrush of thorny vines. They scratched at my ankles,
drawing blood as I hurried my pace. Panic flooded through
me. I called out for Byron or Shelley, but no one responded.
Black clouds gathered above – thick and heavy – and I grew
frightened.

I kept running.

Lightning flashed across the sky and thunder rolled in with
deep, pounding waves. I covered my ears and halted, not
knowing whether I should go back.

The storm's ferocity grew into a violent dance of light and
booming explosions.

Then rain began to fall in cold, hard sheets, and I sank to
my knees.

I could not go on.

I heard Byron call out my name, and I struggled to my
feet. I moved in that direction, feeling more surefooted on the
path as I grew closer to the sound of his voice.

Finally, I emerged from the trees and saw him standing in
the open ground with a child at his side, wearing a blue dress,
matching bonnet, and a gold necklace. She smiled.

*Allegra.*

They were waiting for me.

Just then, a jagged streak of lightning hit the space in front of them, and they vanished and were gone forever.

I awoke with a gasp as I realized it was but a dream . . . then a few moments of sadness followed. I rarely dreamed about Allegra, but now that we were drawing closer to Bagnacavallo, she was constantly in my thoughts.

Growing stronger day by day.

As I joined the rest of our little group in the morning room for a light breakfast, I said nothing about the dream, although my muted demeanor elicited a few sidelong glances from Paula and Raphael. Having regained their lively spirits, they finished up and took Georgiana into the courtyard to play in the sun before she was shut up inside the carriage again. Trelawny and I remained alone with our coffee and *fette biscottate.*

'You seem very quiet, Claire. Are you having second thoughts about journeying on after what happened yesterday?' He sat back in his chair, his head tilted to one side, regarding me intently.

I took a sip of my coffee – a deep roast. 'Quite the contrary. I am more resolved than ever to continue on our quest, as long as Georgiana is protected.'

'Agreed. Raphael and I discussed it early this morning, and we proposed that one of us will always have her in sight. There will be no more "incidents," believe me.'

'I do . . . and I, too, will remain on guard.' I set my cup on the table.

He still watched me, eyes flicking over my face. 'Is there something else on your mind?'

Setting my hands in my lap, I looked down at the faint wrinkles that fanned across my fingers in delicate lines. The hands of a lady – or at least those of a woman who had never done hard, manual labor. Not an easy life, but not a grindingly difficult one either. In that, I had been fortunate.

'Claire?'

'Last night I dreamed of Byron during the time we spent together in Geneva. He looked young and handsome – the way I remember him. He was waiting for me at Diodati as I tried to find my way there through a terrible storm. I was lost and desperate yet, somehow, found my way to him. Then I saw he was with Allegra.' I paused, not wanting to relate the next part.

'Was that all?'

I shook my head. 'A bolt of lightning struck, and they disappeared.' My hands clenched, gathering the fabric of my cotton dress. 'As if they never existed.'

'But they did,' Trelawny said with deliberate emphasis.

'Yes, so long ago . . .'

'It may seem that way at times, but in the grand tapestry of life, it was not that far in the past.' He gave a short laugh. 'Perhaps having lived to this age, I see the flow of time in decades, not years. Some of it blurs a bit, but other parts seem even more vivid than when I actually experienced it.'

'I, too, have memories that seem burned into my mind – forever real.' I flexed my fingers again and smoothed down the crumpled dress. 'There was one part of the dream that seemed different, though. When I saw Allegra, she was not wearing the little necklace of carnelians that I had given her. Instead, she wore a tiny horn-shaped pendant on a thin, gold chain . . . the kind Italians wear to protect themselves from the *malocchio* – the evil eye.'

'Ah, the *cornicello* – little horn.' Its significance dawned on him immediately. 'You probably saw someone wearing the charm yesterday and then recreated it in your dream. It is perfectly understandable.'

'But every other time I have dreamed about her, she wore the carnelian necklace – a mother's gift,' I protested. 'And she never removed it while she lived with me.'

Mulling over my words, Trelawny turned meditative in his expression. 'I think it simply means that, like most mothers, you wanted to protect your child, but you could not. No mother could have done so. And now you want to see the place where she supposedly died – find out what happened to her and finally banish the "evil eye" that has hovered over your life.'

'I suppose so.' Casting a doubtful glance toward him, I conceded that everything he said sounded plausible – perhaps even possible. Still, I felt uneasy.

He rose. 'I shall buy you a *cornicello* when we arrive in Ravenna; it will stave off any self-doubt, as well.'

*Double protection.* As a Catholic, I acknowledged that it seemed more appropriate to pray to one of the many saints for safety and security; as a mother, I preferred to confront the *malocchio* from many angles. 'It cannot hurt . . . Raphael keeps one in his pocket.' I drained the last of my coffee and followed him out to the carriage – ready for whatever awaited us.

By midday we arrived at the Convent of San Giovanni near the heart of Bagnacavallo – a small cluster of neoclassical buildings that formed the town center. We stopped in front of the convent, and I scanned the medieval structure with its unremarkable Baroque façade. Such a forbidding exterior. The kind of stern, reclusive appearance that spoke of nuns who rarely traveled outside its walls.

*Poor Allegra.*

Trelawny swung open the carriage door, saying, 'I sent word to the Abbess that we would arrive today, so she should be here to greet us shortly.'

I alighted with Paula and Georgiana at my side. From my niece's expression, I could tell that she, too, found the convent a bit too cold and austere for her taste. Her arm slid around Georgiana in a shielding embrace.

Although the day had turned fine with a bright, sapphire-tinted sky, I found my focus on the convent's stark exterior. It lacked trees and flowers – and all the beautiful touches of nature that gave life to stone and brick. Just bare spaces.

'I cannot believe my daughter lived here – such a lifeless place,' I muttered to Trelawny.

'Perhaps only on the outside,' he replied. 'When Shelley visited Allegra in 1821, he told me she seemed happy and much improved from the fearful child she had become in Ravenna. She even played a prank on the nuns by ringing the church bells to summon them from their cells before he departed. They were not cross with her at all.'

I sniffed. 'He told me much the same story, though I am not sure how much he embellished it to pacify me.'

Before I could say more, a plump woman about my age appeared in a head-to-toe black habit. She apologized profusely to me in Italian for her lateness.

'*Sono appena arrivato qui,*' I responded, assuring her that I had just arrived.

'*Bene.*' She then inclined her head toward each member of our little group and patted Georgiana's curls. '*Bella bambina.*'

A glow emanated from the Abbess's small-featured, wrinkled face – compelling in its warmth – and I found some of my initial impressions of the nunnery shift slightly.

Trelawny did the introductions, and then the Abbess ushered us inside. As I listened to her explain the origin of the convent in English, I found myself intrigued to hear that it had begun in the fourteenth century as a monastery and was later damaged in an earthquake in the 1600s and then abandoned. The Capuchin nuns acquired the property a century after that and opened a boarding school for daughters of noble Italian families. Grudgingly, I had to admit the convent had a distinguished background.

Its hushed interior also had a stately quality with wood-beamed ceilings, white walls, and religious artwork. A place of worship and beauty.

Not at all what I expected.

'Do you still accept young ladies as students?' Paula asked, keeping a tight hold on Georgiana's hand as we passed a delicate china statuette that sat atop a table.

'Only a few. The convent education does not seem as fashionable as it was in the past,' she said with a shrug as she led us down a long corridor. 'Are you inquiring for your daughter?'

'Oh, no.' She edged Georgiana closer. 'I prefer to have her with me.'

The Abbess smiled and nodded.

'I can see why your numbers have dwindled . . . It is a bit isolated.' I took in the small, square stained-glass windows positioned in a neat row above the corridor's archways. Sunlight filtered through the opaque glass with slanted beams against the opposite wall, providing only faint illumination.

'Though Ravenna is only twenty kilometers to the east,' Raphael added, trailing behind us.

*A half-day's ride at most.*

Yet, unlike Shelley, Byron never visited Allegra in the

convent, not even after I repeatedly asked him to do so. I never understood how he could abandon her so completely . . . but the situation was more complicated than I knew.

'Signora?' The Abbess held open the door to her office.

Quickly, I moved inside with Trelawny, but Raphael and Paula demurred, asking instead if they could take Georgiana outside to the interior garden for her to play.

She gave her permission, probably sensing, as I did, that Paula did not want her young daughter to hear the adult conversation that was about to take place. I could not blame her.

Once inside the large office, the Abbess seated herself behind a carved desk as Trelawny and I slid into two high-backed chairs across from her. A gilded cross, suspended from the ceiling, loomed behind her as the sole wall decoration, other than a painting of the Madonna holding the baby Jesus in her lap. The room smelled of incense – deep and pungent.

'Signor Trelawny did not state the purpose of your visit,' she began, folding her hands atop the desk. 'But I assume it has something to do with your daughter, Allegra.'

My breath caught in the back of my throat. 'You are most frank, *Madre.*'

'After running this convent for many years, I have found there is no point in being indirect. The role demands candidness.' She met my glance squarely, but her tone was gentle. 'And that I follow the will of God in all matters.'

I crossed myself.

*Per grazia di Dio.*

Trelawny merely raised a brow. 'I cannot claim to know divine intent, but I believe that some force guides us to our better selves if we allow it, which is why *we* are here – to find the truth.'

'Indeed, I wish for that, as well.' The Abbess shifted slightly in her chair as if she was ready to hear a confession. 'And to assist you in any way that I can.'

Taking in a deep breath, I began to explain the incredible shifts in my life over the last fortnight, including the discovery that Allegra might have survived the typhus epidemic that swept through the convent all those years ago. The Abbess's face registered very little reaction until I mentioned the murder of Father Gianni; at that point, she visibly started, causing me to pause in my story. 'Did you know him?'

She shook her head.

'I ask because you seemed to recoil when I touched on his death,' I pressed.

'Only the manner of his death took me aback. When a priest is killed inside his own basilica, it sends shudders through my soul. A holy man should be seen as sacred even by those who are not believers.' Her lips murmured a brief Italian prayer. 'But I need not tell you that since it seems as if you also lost a dear friend in him.'

The image of his face flashed in my memory, compassion radiating from his eyes. 'I did. He taught me about love and forgiveness – and brought me to the light of faith. I shall always honor him in my heart.' As I spoke the words, I also heard Matteo's warning echo through my mind: *Father Gianni was not all that he seemed.*

My priest. My advisor. My salvation.

Was it possible he deceived me?

'A man can have no greater praise,' the Abbess pronounced solemnly.

Trelawny gave a guttural snort of impatience. 'I appreciate your sentiments over the priest's nobility, but we came here to learn if you sent Father Gianni any information about Allegra,' he said. 'At Signora Clairmont's behest, he wrote to you a few weeks ago, asking about her daughter, and the day he died, he was supposed to relate some information that he had found—'

'But I received no inquiry,' she interjected, blinking with bafflement. 'Nor, as I said, was I ever acquainted with Father Gianni. When I received Signor Trelawny's note about your visit yesterday, it was the first time I had ever heard that Allegra Byron's mother still lived in *Italia*. *Firenze* is a world away from Bagnacavallo, and we live very quiet lives here.'

I stared at her, speechless.

*Truly?*

Father Gianni had never sent her a letter?

He *had* deceived me.

I felt Trelawny squeeze my arm in reassurance, but it was

cold comfort as I stammered, 'I . . . I must say that I am astonished. It is not the behavior of the man I knew. When I appealed to him in Florence to intervene on this matter, he promised me that he would write to you. And I believed him – there was no earthly reason to doubt his honesty.' Was it possible that yet another person whom I held so dear had misled me? Byron. Trelawny. And now Father Gianni. All of them.

'I am sorry,' she said quietly. 'Could it be that his note was lost along the way?'

'Perhaps.' More likely that Matteo had spoken the truth that day at Le Murate. What an irony. And a painful one, no less. Father Gianni's lessons in charity had been as hollow as his vow to help me.

Slumping back in my chair, I let this new reality settle into my heart. Even though I had made my way through the world with my instinct to survive, I always believed in the kindness of those who befriended me. Perhaps that had been my greatest mistake . . .

'The post *can* be slow and unreliable,' Trelawny added, though I knew it was simply to assuage my feelings. 'Even if Father Gianni's letter is still en route, we are here now to conduct our inquiry about Allegra in person, but I will let Claire make the appeal.'

The Abbess inclined her head.

Trelawny nudged me gently to proceed, but I found myself at a loss to speak. It all felt a bit futile right now. Maybe the tides were turning against me in this part of the journey, so much so that I might never reach the shore that I so desired.

'Claire?' he prompted.

Instead of responding, I fixed my glance on the painting of the Madonna and the Christ-child who sat in her lap, nestled in the folds of her scarlet dress. Mary's eyes half shut, she gazed down at her baby with love and sadness. His youth would soon be gone as he grew into a man and, even worse, he would be taken from her far too soon. But he smiled, holding out a strawberry plant sprig with two leaves – the Father and Holy Ghost. An offering that could not be denied. He would be restored to her in ways that she could not even dream.

*The Trinity of Hope.*

She never gave up. Nor would I.

Taking a few moments to compose myself, I began on a note of appeal. 'Considering what I have learned recently about my daughter's supposed death, I want to prevail upon you to open the convent's records from April 1822 – if they still exist – so I can see if something about the typhus epidemic had been altered to hide her true fate . . . I ask you this as a Catholic and a mother.'

The Abbess remained immobile for a few moments, her hands still folded on the desk. Then she finally replied, 'You realize what you are asking? For many reasons, all of our records are sealed for the sake of the privacy of the young women who attended the convent as students. Many powerful Italian families placed females here because they did not want their identities revealed. Not everyone is as open about a child's paternity as you, Signora Clairmont.'

I knew what she meant: illegitimate offspring were enrolled here – and came from even the best families.

Trelawny leaned forward. 'If I may add my voice to hers, Byron himself told me that Allegra survived the typhus—'

'And you waited all this time to reveal it?' Her brows rose a fraction.

'Only because he made me promise never to tell anyone, and I followed his wishes for my entire life – until I knew it was simply a matter of time before the whole truth came out. But I freely admit that I lied.' Regret threaded through his voice. 'That is my sin, and I must live with it. But now I have a chance to make it right again.'

'Do you think Lord Byron himself might have been the one who lied?' the Abbess queried. 'Perhaps he blamed himself for his daughter's death and simply created a fiction to assuage his conscience. Grief can cause strange behavior.'

'No,' Trelawny responded swiftly and firmly. 'He spoke the truth about Allegra. I believe it with every part of my being. As soldiers who faced death together, we had a bond that went deep . . . knowing that each day might be our last. He told me during his final days as all men do when there may not be much time left.'

'Like Matteo,' I added.

His mouth thinned. 'I hate to admit it, but yes – like Matteo. He knew he was going to commit suicide, so that was his last act to try to redeem his soul. I suppose we must at least honor his attempt to ease his conscience.'

'But in doing so, he committed an offense against God by taking his own life.' The Abbess's eyes hardened slightly – a glint that reflected a wall of rigidity. 'I fear he will face damnation for that transgression—'

'I disagree with you on this matter, Madre,' Trelawny cut in with an equally tough stare. 'If a man like Matteo wishes to remove himself from this world, I think he should do it and rid the rest of us of his heartless evil. In my years on the battlefield, I saw many men like him, and there is no changing their nature. They enjoy giving rein to the kind of darkness that most of us shield ourselves from with our belief in morality – however fragile. It keeps us on the path of justice. But they never fight for a cause; they fight because they enjoy killing. I did what I had to do, but I never liked it.'

She shook her head. 'While a man lives, there is always hope.'

Before Trelawny could continue, I spoke up. 'Perhaps we could settle this spiritual matter at another time since I am still waiting for an answer to my original request: can you open the convent's records, Madre? As you see, I am not a young woman, and I would like to have some closure before it is too late. I may not have too many years left, and I want to know what happened.' I paused. '*Please*, do this for me.'

When she did not respond, I realized that no entreaty would dissuade her from the rules and regulations that she had embraced as a bride of Christ. I gazed up at the Madonna again. As a mother, *she* would have granted my request.

*Ave, O Maria, piena di grazia . . .*

'I shall grant your request, Signora Clairmont,' the Abbess said. 'Whether Father Gianni sent a letter to me about your daughter or not, I believe he probably intended to do what he felt was best for you. I believe that a mother should know the fate of her own child. It may take a few hours. All the convent documents are kept in the cellar and I will sort through them this afternoon – if you can wait.' She stood, her back straight and tall as if she were one of the statues of blank-faced saints that we had passed along the hallway. Not made of stone. But the strength of compassion.

I sighed in relief, giving thanks to the Madonna for answering my plea.

'You seem to be riveted on the painting.' She cast a momentary glance over her shoulder. 'It is beautiful, is it not?'

'*Bella*,' I echoed in Italian. 'The artist must have been moved by the subject matter to create such a beautiful rendering of the Madonna and Child – the use of texture and color is breathtaking. It looks quite old . . . perhaps some unknown Renaissance painter?'

'More like an excellent reproduction,' she corrected me. 'It hung in this very place when I arrived at the convent, and I was told that one of our students had painted it as a gift to the nuns who taught her. Naturally, I could not move it. During my tenure as Abbess, I have taken great comfort in its beauty. There is such a glow of holiness in every stroke of the brush.'

'Indeed.' I smiled. 'It is also a testament to the loving guidance that the teachers provided to her. She was most fortunate to have been educated here – as was Allegra.' There. I had admitted it aloud. Perhaps my anger with Byron had prevented me from seeing that the convent could provide her not only with an education but with kindness. I had not wanted to see the reality of that fact, but I did now.

My initial impression shifted even more so.

'May we tour the convent grounds while you search the records?' Trelawny asked in a brusque tone, obviously still somewhat irritated that the Abbess had not agreed with his assessment of Matteo's character. He never was one to back down from an argument. Or change his position.

'*Certamente*.' She gestured toward a low-beamed side door. 'If you leave through that portal and follow the passage, it will take you toward the courtyard and the gardens. You might also want to see the Chiesa di San Giovanni – the church connected to the convent. It dates back to the fourteenth century and has four chapels, one with a main altar of rare, colored marble – beautiful.'

He inclined his head. 'You are most obliging.'

I rose to accompany him, but the Abbess held up her hand.

'Signora Clairmont, I thought you might like to see the room where Allegra stayed while she lived here – it is not in use presently.'

My heartbeat quickened, but I remained still. Could I manage a visit to Allegra's room without dissolving into tears? Stand in the space where she had awakened every morning, slept every evening, and drawn her last breath on this earth – or so I thought. *My sweet daughter.* Of course I wanted to see the room. With all my heart. Its four walls had contained her presence within, if only for a short time, and perhaps something of her spirit lingered in the air like the perfume of a flower that once bloomed. Delicate. Soft. Just beyond the reach of the senses. I could never let go of wanting to inhale that scent one more time.

At least I could see her in my mind's eye.

Turning to Trelawny, I said, 'I shall join the rest of you after I see her room.'

'Are you sure, Claire?' He waited.

'Yes.'

'Then I shall accompany you—'

'No, I must do this alone.' I took one final, brief glance at the Madonna, her face lit with maternal love. 'It is a farewell of sorts . . . I will be fine. Truly.'

He stared at me for a few moments then exited through the door, ducking low to avoid the wooden beam across the top.

'Come.' The Abbess ushered me into the main corridor and up a small flight of stairs.


*Palazzo Guiccioli, Ravenna, Italy*
*January 2, 1821*


*Allegra's Story*


Papa seems to be nervous all the time, staying up late at night when Pietro is here. And I never see the contessa anymore. Papa told me she is staying with her family outside of Ravenna and that the weather was too cold for her to travel, but I do not think he is telling me the truth.

Something else is happening because I am rarely allowed to leave the palazzo.

I can feel the tension all around me.

And I sometimes hear shots outside at night.

Papa's carriage driver disappeared and, afterwards, the other servants began to speak in muted tones in the hallways. Always in Italian. But I can understand them. They are afraid Papa will be arrested, and they will be implicated in his crimes. But he is not a *traditore.*

Everyone seems afraid.

Except for Tita. He fears nothing and no one. And he never lets me out of his sight now, sometimes sleeping outside my room with a gun at his side.

A few days ago, I heard Papa discussing with Tita something about a convent in Bagnacavallo, but they abruptly stopped talking when I approached. I do not know what that means, but I hope that Papa does not want me to go there. He says I need to be in a school for young ladies so I can marry well, but I do not want to leave him.

I would die if I had to part from Papa again.

# SEVEN

'And love shall be his torment; but his grief
Shall make an immortality of tears . . .'

*The Prophecy of Dante*, III, 101–102

*The Convent of San Giovanni, Bagnacavallo, Italy
July 1873*

The air grew warm and stifling as the Abbess led me down a narrow hallway on the second floor of the convent.

Near the end of the passage, I saw a slender not-so-young woman with dark hair and pale skin, holding her Bible and rosary in hand, coming toward us. She gave a greeting in Italian and moved on, her skirt whispering along the floor with a quiet flutter. No one followed her. 'We have only a handful of teachers here during the summer – mostly ones who live in Bagnacavallo . . .'

'I was a governess as well – not only in Italy, but Russia,' I commented, noting that the windows along the north side of the hallway were closed and latched tightly. 'Moscow was a cold place, but the Zotoffs – my employers – treated me as if I were part of their family . . . and their daughter, Betsy, became a friend to me even after I left Russia. I corresponded with her for many years.'

'No doubt being around children gave you great joy.' She stopped in front of an open door. 'I will leave you here then . . . please stay as long as you like.'

'*Grazie.*'

As she moved off, a sudden thought occurred to me: 'How do you know this was Allegra's room? Her stay here was so long ago.'

She hesitated and spoke without turning around. 'I was told by the previous Abbess when I arrived. She was elderly then, her memory failing somewhat, but she recollected that the English poet's daughter lived in this chamber – nothing beyond that, though.' The Abbess then hurried off, promising to send word as soon as she located any record of Allegra's days at the convent.

I could only hope that she would find something . . . anything.

I took a few moments to compose myself at the threshold of Allegra's room and, slowly, entered. As I strolled around the small space, first impressions touched me – white walls adorned with a small etching of Jesus Christ, a narrow bed with a neatly tucked-in quilt, and a dark wooden cabinet with several drawers in the lower half. Nothing remarkable. Nothing personal to suggest these walls had housed Allegra.

As her name floated through my thoughts, I tried to summon an image of my daughter reading a book in the corner or kneeling to say her prayers at night. Hear the sound of her childish laughter as it trailed through the solemn quiet of the convent. Touch the fabric of her dresses that her papa had had made of the finest Venetian silk. But I could not bring any of these visions to life.

It seemed empty.

And, strangely, I felt numb.

So different from my visit to Bagni di Lucca when it breathed memories from the past time and place that I had shared with Mary and Shelley. But the convent held no such recollections for me. I could not reach back into my psyche and find any deep emotion tied to this tiny cell. Perhaps Byron had been right when he mused on memory . . .

> All that mem'ry love the most
> Was once our only hope to be:
> And all that hope adored and lost
> Hath melted into memory.

It was inevitable, I suppose, that some things faded into a cupboard, carefully wrapped and tucked away in a neglected nook of lost imaginings, but I would never see it as delusion – more like moving into a fresh new room in the same house. Some precious objects had to be put out of sight or they would clutter every inch of every space. Just not my daughter.

Then again, it was always possible the Abbess had been wrong about this being Allegra's room since I never knew its location.

Sighing, I noted the sunlight slant through the small window, beaming across the bed with a rich glow. To see the courtyard garden, Allegra would have had to stand on a chair, but, knowing her stubborn will, she would have done so at every opportunity. Her portal to the outside world. The glass at the top formed a cloudy, diamond-shaped pattern, but the lower half was a single, clear pane which provided a wide and open view of the flowers and cypress trees below. Much like her father, she had loved nature.

But this room had little to offer me beyond the fact that Allegra once lived here. Then my glance fell upon a scratch on the lower right side of the windowpane. Several rough, jagged lines that seemed to form . . . letters. I edged closer and leaned down, making out the initials, 'AB.' My hand went to my mouth, stifling a small cry.

*Allegra Byron.*

In that moment, I had a flash of her face, blue eyes sparkling with mischievous intent as she scratched her initials on the window. She giggled . . . and I listened as the sound swirled around me – finally, I could see her again and hear her laughter. My child. She had left this mark. Sinking on to the bed, I let the knowledge sink in. Then I smiled. Could anything be more delightful than envisioning Allegra doing something endearing? The child of my heart.

I sat there for some time, quiet and still, savoring the moment. Whatever I learned from the convent records, at least I had *this* memory to sustain me.

'Aunt Claire?' Paula hovered in the doorway, watching me intently. 'You were gone so long that I grew worried. Trelawny told us that the Abbess brought you upstairs to your daughter's . . . room. Are you all right?'

'Better than ever now that I have seen it.' I patted the bed,

and Paula took her place next to me. 'It seemed a rather
cold and forbidding place at first – until I spied something.'
I pointed to the 'AB' initials etched on the pane. Paula moved
toward the window and, after recognizing what the letters
signified, she turned to me, her eyes wide with surprise.

'Do you think that Allegra . . . did that?'

'I do.'

Paula traced the letters with her index finger. 'The cuts have
smoothed down with the passage of time, almost not even
visible at this point. One would have to have been looking for
the marking.' She turned to me. 'Did the Abbess show it to
you?'

'No – she never mentioned it,' I responded. 'We must tell
her when she returns.'

'Do you think she will find anything in the records to help
us? After all these years, I cannot imagine that someone did
not notice a discrepancy about Allegra's death. It seems
unlikely . . .' Paula faltered, seemingly hesitant to say more.

'But not impossible.' I held out a hand to her. 'Let us take
this as a sign that we were meant to travel to the convent so
I could see an image of my daughter that I have never seen
before. It gladdened my heart, and whatever happens next, at
least I will have that.'

She briefly raised my hand to her cheek. 'You are so right,
Aunt.'

'Sometimes a journey does not lead where one would think,'
I said, half to myself. 'But I have never regretted setting out
on a new road – it may lead to some discovery which is totally
unexpected. Even at my age, I find the possibility intriguing.'
I rose from the bed. 'Now, let us join Trelawny and Raphael
. . . they are probably at their wits' end being in sole charge
of Georgiana.'

'I thought you said Trelawny had children of his own?'

'Oh, my dear, *he* was never the one to care for them – that
was the responsibility of his three wives. I am afraid most
men, as you know, are not exactly skilled in child-rearing.'

'Indeed,' she readily agreed. 'Even Raphael seems hapless
at times when it comes to Georgiana.'

'But he does try to help you and he loves Georgiana – that

is truly what counts.' I rose and glanced around the room once more with a deep sigh. 'It is very difficult for a woman to raise a child alone; while I did not want to give up Allegra, sending her to Byron and eventually the convent gave her a much better life that I could ever have provided for her—'

'You do not know that,' Paula protested. 'It was a painful choice, but you did what you thought was best for her.'

'Perhaps . . . there are so many unknowns when it comes to how fate might have changed our lives – one small turn around a different corner, one altered decision – I cannot say how it would have turned out.' I linked my arm through hers. 'Come along, there is nothing more for us to see here.' And with that, I drew her out of the room, leaving that vision of Allegra behind.

It was time to move on.

As we exited, I thought I heard a tiny giggle once more, trailing us into the hallway. She would always be with me.

We made our way toward the courtyard, not saying much beyond a brief observation about the pristine state of the convent – the Abbess seemed to run a tight ship when it came to cleanliness being next to Godliness. A quality that had always seemed to elude me. In fact, I preferred a bit of mess here and there; it made life interesting.

Once we emerged, I blinked in the bright afternoon sunlight as it glinted off the rich brown buildings of Bagnacavallo just visible outside the walls, no doubt bustling with the kind of vibrancy not present inside the convent.

Too quiet for me. Having grown used to living in Florence, I preferred the constant hum of activity.

Paula and I strolled through the herb and flower garden toward a stand of cypress trees where Trelawny held Georgiana high in his arms so she could pick a small, brownish-gold cone from its branches. Raphael guided her arm, murmuring words of encouragement in Italian and English.

'I may need to revise what I just said about men and child-rearing,' I murmured as we approached them. 'It appears they are doing just fine.'

'Surprisingly so,' Paula responded.

Once Georgiana had completed her task, Trelawny set her

down again, and she dashed toward us, her curls flying behind her as she chattered away in Italian to her mama.

Trelawny turned to me. 'Was your visit upstairs . . . successful?'

'And more.' Smiling, I glanced up at Allegra's window. 'Somehow I think I found her again – at least the girl she was when she lived here.' Moving toward an iron bench in the middle of the courtyard, I noticed a profusion of rosemary bushes with small, blue flowers – the 'dew of the sea,' symbolizing remembrance. So fitting, because I would always recall this day. 'Did you hear anything from the Abbess?'

'Not yet,' Raphael said. 'Considering the convent's age and the number of students who lived here over the years, it may be a while before she finishes her search through the records.'

I slid on to the bench. 'Do we still have time, Trelawny?'

He nodded. 'We are only hours from Ravenna, but I will send word to the Al Cappello that we may arrive late in the day. I also need to check on a few details with my contact here at the Piazza Nuova – it is only a few blocks away, so I should not be long.' He gave a little bow and headed out through an open archway.

After he left, Paula queried, 'While we wait, would you like to see the Chiesa di San Giovanni, Aunt Claire? Georgiana was too restless to take inside the church – and I would like to see the marble altar.'

'By all means you go, but I think I shall remain here. The day is too fine to be indoors.'

She paused. 'Are you certain it is not too warm?'

'Absolutely.' I reached into my bag and pulled out Byron's memoir. 'And I have plenty to occupy myself.'

After Paula asked once again, she finally strolled off with Raphael and Georgiana reluctantly in tow. Slightly relieved to be left alone, I leaned back against the hard iron bench, absently noting the wild rose vines that grew around its legs. Then I put on my spectacles and flipped to the page where I had stopped reading, when Byron stood vigil over his wounded carriage driver through the night in Ravenna . . .

\*     \*     \*

*The danger has passed with Guido – he will live.*

*By the early morning hours, he had improved enough to be moved to his family's farm outside the city. After his father and brother smuggled him out of the palazzo, I still could not sleep. I paced the room, wrote annoyed letters to all my correspondents in England who rarely answered my repeated requests for news of London, then checked on Allegra at least half a dozen times.*

*Exhausted, I finally dozed off in my study, pistol in hand, only to be awakened a few hours later by Tita.*

*He told me rumors had been swirling around Ravenna all night that a mob of Austrian sympathizers intended to march on the palazzo and take me prisoner. But as they gathered near the Battistero degli Ariani, one of them had been stabbed by the Carbonari in an ambush – then the rest disbanded.*

*I refrained from asking who had wielded the knife, noting that one of Tita's short blades, which he kept in his sash, was missing.*

*The call to arms would be soon.*

*Allegra needed to leave Ravenna.*

*Much as I do not wish to part from her, I know it is best. If I am arrested – or worse – she would be at great risk.*

*I dispatched Tita to the nearby Convent of San Giovanni to contact the Capuchin nuns. She would be safe there.*

*Claire will not like it . . .*

Slowly, I closed the memoir.

No, I did not like it, but at least now I understood it. But why had Byron withheld the truth from me? If I had known about the dire situation in Ravenna, I would not have been filled with bitter disappointment over what I believed to be his mistreatment of our daughter and disregard for my feelings when he placed her in the convent. He could have restored himself so easily in my esteem, yet he chose to let me continue to think badly of him.

Then again, Byron always let people think what they wanted about his true character, never bothering to reveal what lay inside the hard shell of disillusionment that he presented to the world. He had his loyal retainers like Tita and Fletcher. The rest could judge as they saw fit. Most people would want others to know about their good deeds, yet Byron hid them.

Slipping the memoir back in my bag, I glanced up again at Allegra's window. Did *she* know how much her father loved her, even in the face of revolution? And how much her mother missed her beyond that? If she was still alive, I could share all of this with her.

*My darling girl.*

Transferring my gaze to the clear blue sky, I spied a lone cloud drift past the sun – one tiny shadow in the endless expanse that stretched above me. Raising my hand as if to brush it off into a far horizon, I heard Paula's voice as they approached.

Then I caught sight of the Abbess emerging from the convent.

She had found something. I knew it.

My heart pounding, I stood quickly and moved toward her at the moment Paula and Raphael returned with Georgiana.

Trelawny must have been delayed, but I could not wait.

'I apologize that it took me so long to find the records about your daughter,' the Abbess began as she held out a large book with frayed leather edges and a faded, gold-embossed stamp of *1822* on the front. 'These old volumes were stacked in a corner in a haphazard pile behind some wooden crates—'

'What did you find?' I cut in eagerly.

She opened the book carefully, brushing off the dust as she pointed at one yellowed page. 'I am afraid it is not good news. On this date of the twentieth of April 1822, it lists six names of young girls who died of the typhus.'

I scanned the names and saw . . . *Allegra Byron.*

My shoulders sagged. 'But that does not mean she actually died. Byron told Trelawny that he fabricated her demise—'

'If so, I am certain there would have been a notation to show where she had been taken – a place, a name . . . something,' she continued. 'As I asked before, is it possible that Byron lied to Trelawny?'

'No – he did not lie to me,' Trelawny declared as he

reappeared in the courtyard. 'All that means is the convent record was forged.'

The Abbess slammed the book shut. 'Are you suggesting that one of our religious order lied about a child's death?'

I felt Paula and Raphael tense.

'Anything is possible,' he said, 'especially if one of the nuns felt she was protecting Allegra from harm. I am not saying it was an immoral act – indeed, it may have been the most ethical choice, given the situation.'

'I have nothing more to say to you, Signor.' The Abbess's mouth tightened into a thin line. 'You may remain in the courtyard to pray, Signora Clairmont, but then I must ask you to leave. I cannot help you further.' She spun on her heel and strode away.

I stared at her retreating figure in bafflement. 'That seemed like a dismissal.'

'Quite rude,' Paula said as we watched the Abbess disappear inside the convent. 'She could have at least entertained the possibility of a forgery.'

'*Si.*' Raphael frowned.

I turned to Trelawny, my hope dimmed as if covered by that tiny cloud that had blocked the sun a few minutes ago. 'You are certain that Byron told you the truth when he said Allegra survived?'

'I am,' he said without hesitation.

'Then we must follow a different avenue because I do not think we will find anything to help us in our quest here.' Taking in a deep breath, I summoned my resolve again. 'Someone in Ravenna may be able to provide information.'

'I can almost guarantee it,' Trelawny promised. 'When I was in Bagnacavallo, I received news from my contact in Ravenna that an important person has agreed to see us tomorrow.'

'Who?' I raised my brows, waiting.

'Teresa Guiccioli.'

I simply stared at him in amazement. 'She still lives?'

He nodded.

Was it possible that the woman who supplanted me in Byron's affections had survived all these years?

If so, she was the one person who might know what actually happened in Ravenna all those years ago – a witness to Bryon's hidden activities with the Carbonari. And a source of truth about Allegra.

'We must see her,' I urged, feeling that cloud dissipate into the clear skies of faith and promise, illuminating the path before us.

Toward Byron's last mistress – Teresa Guiccioli.


*Convent of San Giovanni, Bagnacavallo, Italy*
*January 19, 1821*

*Allegra's Story*

I felt cold.

Standing in the convent courtyard under one of the old cypress trees, I looked up at its branches shaped into a point at the top. Stretching up like a spear into the sky. Straight and strong. All of the oak and chestnut trees in Italy turned bare and gray during winter, but the cypress never lost its color. It always looked like spring, with branchlets sprouting tiny brownish-gold cones, even though the season was a long way off.

Where was Papa? He had been inside with the old Abbess for hours.

When we arrived, she had welcomed us warmly. Even though she seemed very old, with skin wrinkled like parchment, I could see she was charmed by Papa, prattling on about how the nunnery was built of Tuscan clay and had been damaged in an earthquake years ago. I stifled a yawn. She then handed me over to Sister Anna – a nun with olive skin and dark, serious eyes.

But I had grown fidgety, so she escorted me out to the courtyard, and when I jested that its barren, wintery garden looked haunted, she simply smiled and urged me to play near the cypress trees because its wood was used to make the cross of Jesus and could ward off demons. *Questo non è affatto vero* – not true. Tita had always told me the tree had the magic

Sud Italia in its being. He gave me a little pendant that he had carved from the bark into an Italian horn, a *cornicello* to protect against the *malocchio* – evil eye. I put it on a silver chain and always wore it under my dress.

She promised to return quickly after prayers.

I want to go home . . . back to Ravenna.

This convent feels like a prison after living with my papa in his palazzo.

I pulled my heavy woolen shawl tighter against the winter wind that blew in from the west.

'*Buongiorno.*' A girl about my age with long red curls and pale skin skipped toward me, then stopped and curtsied. 'I am Chiara.'

I did the same as I introduced myself.

'Are you going to be a student here?' she queried.

Shaking my head vigorously, I explained that my Papa would never allow that to happen.

She did not respond.

Suddenly feeling a sense of uncertainty, I pulled out my little pendant and held it close, explaining the magic powers behind the *cornicello*.

'You will not need that here.' Her face took on a happy glow. 'The Madonna watches over us.'

She must have noticed my puzzled expression because she began to tell the story of Mother Mary and the Bambino. As I listened politely, I tucked the *cornicello* inside my dress again. Perhaps I would not need it after all.

'I was going to watch the old man from the village who weaves baskets out of straw – he has a cart just outside the wall, even in the winter.' Chiara pointed to an open archway. 'Do you want to join me? If you are very quiet while he works, he will give you a *fritole*.'

I clapped in excitement and started to follow her when Sister Anna hurried out of the convent portico and exclaimed, 'You must stay on the convent grounds, Allegrina. Your papa will not be long.'

My spirits drooped as I watched Chiara depart.

Sister Anna held out her hand. 'Come along, it is too cold to be outside.'

'*Si.*' I let her lead me indoors where we waited in an empty hallway for what seemed like an eternity.

When I finally spied Papa, I gave a cry of relief and ran toward him.

I never wanted to see this place again.

# EIGHT

'Pleasure shall, like a butterfly new caught,
Flutter her lovely pinions . . .'

*The Prophecy of Dante*, III, 115–116

*Convent of San Giovanni, Bagnacavallo, Italy*
*July 1873*

I could scarcely believe it as I listened to Trelawny explain that when he had been making inquiries in Ravenna about members of the Gamba family who might help us in our quest, he learned that Teresa still lived – and resided outside the city.

An unexpected turn of fate, to say the least.

'But she must be quite old,' Paula blurted out, then her face flushed as she realized the import of her words. 'Pardon me, Aunt . . . I did not mean to imply anything that would reflect on *your* age. You are truly the most remarkable person. I was simply surprised.'

'I take no offense, my dear,' I assured her. 'The truth is I am not young by any means. I, too, was astonished – not so much that Teresa had reached my age, but that I had not heard about it. After all, Florence is not that far from Ravenna.' Through the years, I had often imagined meeting Teresa, trying to understand why Byron had turned to her after me, but I realized no good could come of such an encounter. Shelley told me she had a pleasing sweetness in her manners that Byron found calming, and I contented myself with that explanation.

Of my many qualities, 'sweetness' was never one that I claimed.

'Apparently, la Guiccioli moved back to Italy only recently. She had married the Marquis de Boissy almost twenty years ago and lived quietly in Paris, penning her book about Byron in French. She waited until her husband died before she published her *Recollections of Lord Byron* in France a few years later . . . then I lost track of her as she moved into the realm of the forgotten,' Trelawny said.

*How well I knew that land. Those of us who traveled with the famous often ended up abandoned in its empty terrain.*

I did not intend to read it.

It was too painful.

Georgiana tugged on Raphael's leg as she pointed at another cone nestled high in a cypress tree. He lifted her in his arms, so she could reach one of the branches.

'How many books can be written about a man, even one as famous as Byron?' Paula kept a steadying hand against her daughter's back. 'I could understand someone like Mr Rossetti wanting to buy Aunt Claire's letters for his Shelley biography, but these gossipy "recollections" of every conversation with Byron seem so . . . tawdry.' She paused, the color rushing into her cheeks once again. 'I did not mean *you*, Trelawny – you wrote about war adventures that you shared with Byron – not mere blather.'

He gave a short bow, but the twist to his mouth signaled that he was well aware that Paula's exception of his work seemed hasty and half-hearted.

'Why did *you* not write your own book about Byron?' Raphael inquired of me, edging Georgiana a bit higher. 'You were part of the literary circle and had first-hand observations of his friendship with Shelley . . .'

As his voice trailed off, I stared off briefly into the distance that stretched beyond the convent walls, as I slid on to the bench again. 'The many others who wrote about their recollections of Byron were friends or social acquaintances, such as Thomas Moore or Lady Blessington, but our relationship was more . . . complicated. I always considered what we shared much too personal to reveal to the world—'

'But Teresa Guiccioli left her husband to live openly with Byron – it had to have been a great scandal at the time. If she could write about her love affair with him, so could you,' Paula pressed. 'And Mary wrote that biography of

Shelley even though he was married when he became her lover.'

Smiling sadly, I shook my head. 'Teresa had rank and wealth, and Mary had literary genius – two qualities that protect a woman from brutal public censure. I have neither. And lest you forget, the world we live in has little tolerance for a woman of obscure background who has a child out of wedlock and chooses never to marry. Believe me, if I had written about my relationship with Byron, *I* am one who would have suffered from cruel attacks.' Besides, I could never bring myself to reveal the intimate details of our connection, initiated by my own bold proposition to meet him outside the city for a secret tryst.

In truth, I had been the aggressor in England – and later in Geneva when I arranged for all of us to connect on the shores of Lac Léman. I wanted to be the muse of a great poet, not just one of the many women who drifted through Byron's life, so I had maneuvered myself into his world.

How could I ever write about those stolen moments when Byron made love to me, created poetry about my 'sweet voice,' and vowed to care for our daughter?

Those memories were mine alone.

At least, he had been true to that last promise – in his own fashion.

Paula gave an exclamation of disgust. 'I think it is spectacularly unfair that you are not given the same favored status to write about Bryon. You deserve the opportunity to tell about your life with him, especially now, when it is possible that Allegra did not die—'

'*That* can never be revealed,' Trelawny cut in with a firm voice. 'Whatever propelled Byron to hide her fate needs to remain a secret . . . at least until we know the whole story.'

'I agree – we must be prudent.' I echoed his tone. 'Saying anything at this point could be dangerous to all of us. And, truly, I prefer to keep some parts of my life private, Paula. Telling all does not mean giving the whole story – just one piece of it. All the so-called friends who wrote about Byron had only a glimpse of the man behind the legend: he always knew how to perform what people expected of him. Only a few of us saw the bitter and lonely man in exile . . .' The friends closest to him.

The ones who turned me into an invisible presence from the past – a ghost hovering only in the edges of their lives.

It still rankled.

I could excuse Trelawny for omitting any references to me in his book because he wanted to protect Allegra, but Mary had expunged me in her writings about our circle to create the portrait of a 'moral' life with Shelley. As a widow with a young son, she struggled with poverty, so I understood her motivation only too well, but I found it hard to accept that my own step-sister could be so callous. And history always sided with those whose fame extended beyond their lives like a drama with no end . . . never with the bit players in the wings. That had been my role, and so be it. But I would write the last act.

'I still think it is unjust.' Paula sniffed.

'True, but this is not the time or place to debate literary fair-ness.' Trelawny motioned toward the archway. 'The horse and carriage await outside, and we need to depart if we are to arrive in Ravenna before evening. I can then send a note to Teresa to inquire if she would be willing to see you, Claire.' He ended the sentence on a questioning note.

'I would like to make her acquaintance.' Sitting back, I let my own words sink in. A meeting with Teresa Guiccioli. My nemesis. My rival. But, strangely, also my hope. If there was any chance that she might have some fragment of a recollec-tion about Allegra's fate, I needed to pursue it. 'Should we inform the Abbess of our departure, just for courtesy's sake?'

'Paula and I can let her know.' Raphael lowered Georgiana to the ground, then he offered Paula his arm. After she took it, the three of them strolled toward the convent.

Once they disappeared inside, I looked up at Trelawny, shielding my face from the sun with my hand. 'Do you think Teresa will agree?'

'Yes.' He seated himself next to me, stretching out his long legs in black riding boots in front of him. 'When I knew her in Pisa all those years ago, she seemed a kind woman, and it would be a great unkindness not to see you. The meeting is long overdue . . .'

'Was she . . . pretty?'

He laughed. 'Having had three wives, Claire, I know better than to answer that question.'

'It was a stupid thing to ask – of course she was pretty. Remember what Byron said in *Don Juan*? "I hate a dumpy woman." He would never have been with an unattractive lover.'

'Certainly not,' he said with deliberate emphasis in my direction.

Somewhat mollified, I knew there was nothing to be gained in pursuing this topic – except reviving my youthful vanity. Still, I could remember what it was like to be 'Beauty's daughter' beyond the lines in Byron's poem. 'I am most eager to meet her for myself.'

'Then our visit here is finished. Perhaps we shall find what we seek in Ravenna.' He rose and extended a hand to me. 'The rider who shadowed us on the first part of our journey seems to have disappeared – for now. But after the incident with Georgiana, we need to remain vigilant.'

'Agreed.' I allowed him to assist me as I rose from the bench, and I took one last look at the window of Allegra's room. 'But I found something here that I had lost, so the trip has given me a gift that I never expected.'

For an instant, I embraced Allegra in my heart before I turned away.

'I am truly happy to hear it.' He drew me toward the archway. 'It is unfortunate that the Abbess was not exactly cooperative.'

'No, but you have found Teresa was still alive. That could be . . . enlightening.' I refrained from pointing out that *he* had offended the Abbess by suggesting that one of her Capuchin order may have forged the convent's records.

As we emerged from the convent walls, I spied the carriage and Trelawny's horse, and while the street seemed quiet with only an occasional passer-by, I felt reassured that he would be riding next to us as we traveled to the end of our journey. And he was right: we had to remain watchful on such unfamiliar terrain.

It was a long, flat road to Ravenna and, as I had seen thus far, anything could happen.

\* \* \*

The trip, in fact, proved to be uneventful, as Trelawny had suggested. Few carriages passed us on the road, and after only two hours, we drove into the heart of Ravenna. Though a stranger to this city, I found it seemed oddly familiar after reading Byron's *confessione.* Typical narrow cobblestone streets. Brown brick buildings. Charming piazzas. Much smaller than Firenze, it had an old-fashioned, elegant appeal.

I could see why Byron found it to be one of his favorite places.

The carriage halted in front of a classically styled palazzo in warm shades of terracotta. As we alighted, I noted a small brass plate near the front entrance that bore the hotel's name: *Al Cappello.* The Hat. A classic name for Italian hotels, yet this one was certainly a step above our usual lodging.

'Do not worry, Claire,' Trelawny said as he dismounted his horse. 'It is well within our budget. The owner is quite a devotee of Byron's poetry and was easily persuaded to offer us rooms at a considerably reduced price when he heard he and I were friends.'

*Of course.*

Trelawny and Raphael saw to the luggage as Paula and I ushered a sleepy Georgiana inside. She had missed her afternoon nap and was visibly drooping. As was I. It had been an emotional day, and I needed a cup of tea and time alone to gather my thoughts – and allow myself to reflect on what might occur next.

Perhaps the end of our quest.

I longed for it but also feared it.

Barely half an hour later, I was settled into a spacious, airy suite with coffered ceilings and a sitting room. Thick red brocade curtains adorned the large open windows, a delicate ladies' desk positioned between them. The room smelled old . . . a scent that lingered from the layers of plaster and paint. As I sat quietly and sipped a strong cup of oolong tea, I felt my spirits revive in such a beautiful setting. Paula and Georgiana resided in a similar room next door, with Trelawny and Raphael down the hall.

Events were moving swiftly now – Trelawny had already set out to contact Teresa about a meeting tomorrow.

The church bells rang out six times in the distance – seeming to come from different parts of the city, and I took a moment to say a silent prayer for strength. I would see this through and know that my life had found new meaning. All that I ever had experienced and all that I wanted to know would come together in this time and place.

My glance fell on Byron's memoir where it lay on the tea table. It, too, bore the traces of age with the faded leather cover and yellowed pages. But each of the recordings rose up from inside so vivid and so real that it seemed as if they had occurred only yesterday: Byron entering the Porto Adriana during Christmas time and being halted by the religious procession, cradling a dying man in his arms outside the Palazzo Guiccioli, and fighting an assassin in the woods of Filetto. The images blurred in my mind's eye like a pageant of scenes that both delighted my senses and grieved my heart.

Picking up the memoir, I traced my fingers along Byron's handwriting – jagged and irregular, scrawled across each page. No one had ever seen this *confessione* aside from Trelawny – and now me with a touch that longed to reach beyond the separation of death. Sadly, I could not breech that gap as I skimmed his words . . .

*I took Allegra to see Dante's Tomb this evening, knowing she would not be with me much longer. I wanted her to remember that her papa was once a poet who admired the great Italian bard who was buried in Ravenna.*

*We could not walk the short distance from the Via Cavour to the* Sepolcro di Dante *because it was too dangerous, so Tita called for my carriage and followed closely behind as we moved through the centre of the city. He then stood guard as I led her inside the small domed monument.*

*Hand in hand, we solemnly moved toward the sarcophagus, the dim interior lit by a single votive lamp, kept burning day and night with Tuscan olive oil. It cast a thin, wavering shadow against the bas-relief of Dante reading at a lectern on the far wall.*

*My fellow poet in exile.*

*He knew only too well the pain of losing one's home.*

*But not the pang of giving up one's daughter . . .*

*Silently, we stood in front of Dante's final resting place, and I squeezed Allegra's fingers, whispering, 'Te amo, mia figlia.'*

*'Te amo, Papa.'*

*I recited the Latin epitaph inscribed on the sarcophagus lid, translating the verse by Canaccio as I pointed at the words: '. . . but since my soul left to be a guest in better palaces / and ever more blissfully reached out to its creator's stars / here is enclosed the remains of me – Dante . . .'*

*'Papa, you are not leaving me, are you?' she asked me in Italian.*

*I could answer her truthfully that I was not departing . . .*

I closed my eyes briefly, feeling the tears spill over my cheeks. He had not wanted to surrender her any more than I had, but we both did what we knew was best for our child. Maybe that was the bond that connected us at this point in time: I now understood that we had found a way for our heads to rule our hearts when it came to our daughter. His deep feelings for Allegra could not be doubted; they permeated each and every line of what he recorded in his memoir.

Taking another sip of tea, I pondered those moments when Byron took inspiration from Dante inside the tomb. Now I also understood why he wrote *The Prophecy of Dante*. It was not just his homage to the great poet; it was his way of finding solace in exile when he had to surrender all ties to his homeland – even his daughter.

As I re-read the passage, I realized yet again that Byron had been a lonely man. I had heard only Shelley's accounts of his excesses and reckless behavior when I lived in Florence, and I imagined Byron's life in Ravenna had been similar to Venice: filled with bright gaiety and beautiful women. In fact, it was very different. Certainly, he had Teresa. But much of the time he lived alone in the Palazzo Guiccioli, wistfully fixating on the past and fatefully anticipating the coming revolution.

How wrong I had been about that, too.

Draining the last of my tea in one long, deep swallow, I

needed to breathe in the fresh breeze as it swept in from the nearby coast. Calm my mind and heart. So I let myself out of the room and down the stairs toward the lobby. I smiled at the young woman who stood behind the desk, but she did not see me. Her head was bent, dark hair falling forward, as she focused intently on some documents that lay stacked in front of her. As I emerged into the late-afternoon sunlight, I took in the fruit market next door, with its lush displays of blackberries, apples, and pears, and the little boys playing soldier with wooden swords in the street. Two chattering young women in pale-colored silk dresses nodded and smiled at me as they strolled past. So ordinary and safe. So different from the city teeming in violence that Byron described in his memoir.

I crossed the narrow street and ambled along, taking in the Renaissance-style buildings, neatly kept with freshly painted walls and blooming flowers in pots along the entranceways. Inhaling the soft scent of roses, I glanced up at the street sign and blinked: Via Cavour. I had stumbled on to the street which housed the Palazzo Guiccioli. Quickening my pace, I scanned the address numbers until I found it.

*Via Cavour 41.*

Byron's residence.

The hub of revolution and scene of so much turmoil.

Staring at the rough brown exterior with its green shuttered windows and massive front door, the palazzo seemed little altered from how Byron described it almost fifty years ago, though perhaps a little more well-worn, with tiny cracks in the walls and chipped tiles on the roof. But still a palace in every way. Except now it was simply a quiet building on a semi-deserted street. No trace of anything beyond the commonplace.

Yet it all had happened here.

I imagined Byron kneeling in the snow next to the Austrian soldier who lay dying, gasping out the word 'assassin' as the city erupted in bloodshed and brutal counterattacks. Carbonari plotting in the shadows. Fierce clashes in the night. And in the middle of this tumult was dear Allegra, playing in the courtyard under Tita's watchful eye. Somehow, innocence still flourished in spite of revolution and war.

A miracle.

Glancing toward the Porta Adriana, I noted the last few pedestrians exit Ravenna's oldest part of town through the graceful archway – and realized that I stood alone on the Via Cavour.

A whiff of something savory being cooked nearby drifted my way. Fragrant herbs and pungent spices used in the Italian dishes that I loved. Realizing that it had been hours since I last dined, I turned to make my way back to the Al Cappello and saw a figure approaching out of the corner of my eye, and an oddly primitive warning sounded in my brain. The shadow rider? Had he followed us here? Turning quickly, I caught only a glimpse of a stocky man wearing a hat that hid his face, approaching with rapid steps . . . then I felt a hard thump against my shoulder and I stumbled backwards, almost falling on to the cobblestones when a young woman caught my arm.

With a surprisingly strong grip, she held me up as I steadied myself again; the unknown man disappeared around a corner without breaking his stride.

'*Signora, stai bene?*' she asked, not letting go.

'*Si.*' Straightening my dress with shaky hands, I tried to calm myself and reassure her once again that I was fine. Then I inquired if she had recognized the man. She shook her head as she released my arm.

'The brim of his hat was pulled down too far to see his face, but it seemed as if he went right toward you,' she said in Italian, 'and attempted to knock you down.'

I tried to brush off the comment with a laugh, but I knew it was true: the man had deliberately targeted me on a public street in the center of Ravenna. Taking in a deep breath, I realized it was time to face the fact that we were being followed by someone who was playing a cat-and-mouse game – first shadowing us, then approaching Georgiana in the woods near Vergato, and now attacking me. But never showing his face, never revealing himself.

One thing was certain: he was growing increasingly bold.

By the time the young woman escorted me back to the Al Cappello, we were chatting companionably, trying to distract ourselves, but I knew from the throbbing pain in my shoulder what had really occurred.

I bade her a grateful farewell and slowly moved inside the lobby, finding it deserted. Thanking my good fortune that I did not have to stop and explain where I had gone, I headed up to my room, locking the door behind me. I leaned back against the door and closed my eyes, rubbing my shoulder and trying to remember anything about the man that might have been remarkable. Medium height. Nondescript clothing. Nothing stood out. And with his face hidden by the hat, I could not say whether he was old or young . . . but there was something familiar about him.

'Did you have a nice walk?' Trelawny asked.

Instantly, my eyes fluttered open to see him lounging in my sitting room, arms folded, with a cold, congested expression on his face.

'I assume a servant let you in—'

'With Paula, of course,' he cut in with a harsh tone. 'She just stepped out for a moment to attend to Georgiana.'

'Oh, I see.'

He tilted his head slightly, his eyes narrowing. 'You seem a bit . . . frazzled. Did something happen while you were out?'

'No . . . well, nothing really significant.' Pausing, I knew he would be able to see through any dissembling; it was better to tell him the truth. 'If you must know, a man ran into me on the Via Cavour, but I cannot say for certain if it was an accident or not. The young woman who helped me back to the Al Cappello thought he tried to knock me down, but I am doubtful—'

'For God's sake, Claire, could you be sensible for once in your life?' He heaved himself off the settee and knocked Byron's memoir to the floor, causing the sheets to scatter. 'We have likely been trailed on our entire journey by a man with some kind of evil intent, and you decide to wander the streets *alone*? Are you mad? The least you could have done was ask Raphael or Paula to accompany you.'

'You are right, and, in truth, I think the attack on me was intentional.' Biting my lip, I kicked myself inwardly for my own foolishness. 'I am very sorry to have caused you distress,

Edward. I was wrong to simply wander off from the hotel. I can only plead a momentary weakness caused by this long, emotional day. Forgive me.'

Staring at the ceiling briefly, he sighed. 'I could never hold a grudge against you, even if you try my patience in a hundred ways.' He then bent down and retrieved the pages, slipping them inside the leather cover before handing it to me. 'The entries are probably out of order.'

As I took it from him, he covered my hand with his.

'You never would let me take care of you, even though I have cherished you my entire life. I always knew that Byron had enthralled you completely and totally – I accepted that. But you could have grown to care for me if you had let me into your heart just a little. We shared that one night together in Pisa – and I never asked you to explain why you simply left me after that. But now I am asking. Why did you give me a glimpse of paradise and then expel me?'

'There is nothing to be gained by discussing this—'

'I want to know the truth. Certainly, I have led a rough life and deceived you when I should have explained everything years ago, but I knew, if I did, that you would never speak or write to me again. So I held my tongue and let the lie stretch between us until it was a dark chasm never to be breached. I accept all of that – and more. But I have cleansed my soul and tried to make amends, and you have given me nothing in return. I ask you again in this place and time when the future feels so uncertain: why?'

I tried to pull away from him, clutching Byron's memoir closer, but Trelawny would not let go. 'Truly, I can scarcely recall it.'

'I do not believe you.'

Images of the young Trelawny in Pisa flashed through my mind. Black hair. Dark eyes. Rakish smile.

Oh, I remembered every moment. He had appeared late at night and found me alone at the Casa Galetti after everyone had simply abandoned me . . . I was desolate, knowing that our magic circle of beloved ones had been shattered forever, and I would never know such happiness again. Not bothering even to light candles, I sat in the darkness, listening to the stillness of the warm summer evening near the Arno River.

Trelawny had appeared in the doorway, almost filling the space with his tall, broad shoulders – his handsome face racked by anguish. I did not speak – just led him to my bed chamber where we let our passion fill the emptiness that surrounded us.

Time stopped. Grief stopped. And I felt alive again in his arms when he swept my hair back and showered my face with slow, passionate kisses.

I held nothing back.

In the early dawn, I watched him sleep – his face so youthful in repose. In my own way, I loved him and could so easily have built a life with him, but would that have been fair? He would never be Byron. Never the man who consumed my heart and soul. He would never light my world with his poetry and brilliance.

For that, he would come to hate me.

We had turned to each other for comfort, but that was not enough.

And I had also seen the way he looked at Mary; once she had grieved for Shelley long enough, he would court her himself. I knew it. And I would not be the third wheel in yet another relationship – ever.

I dressed and let myself out of the villa without waking him. Three days later, I traveled to Germany to stay with my brother who then arranged for the governess position in Moscow.

I never mentioned that night again to Trelawny, nor did he ever inquire as to why I left him so abruptly.

It became our secret . . .

'Claire?' he prompted.

Yanking my arm back, I exclaimed, 'All right, then, let us finally put this matter to rest between us. That time in Pisa was devastating – I had lost everyone who was dear to me. I suppose I reached out to you as the one person who would love me, if only for a brief time. But you also loved Mary, and I would not compete with her for your affections.'

'That is not true.'

'You asked her to marry you—'

'Only after you turned me down repeatedly. I wrote to you every day after you disappeared in Pisa – until your brother told me where you had gone and made me swear not to bother you again, until you were ready to contact me.' He paused. 'When you finally wrote to me, you made it clear that you intended us to be friends only, and I fulfilled that role – until now.'

'You certainly found an endless array of wives to assuage your broken heart,' I pointed out with a sarcastic edge to my voice. 'And that would have included Mary if she had been so inclined.'

'That is unfair. By that time, Mary was a widow with a young son – disowned by Shelley's father . . . I only wanted to protect her.'

I raised a brow. 'Is it too much to want you to pine for me – and only me?'

'Probably not, but it is more than a man can give.'

'Obviously.'

Dipping his head, he spoke quietly. 'If you had told me that I had even the slightest chance of winning your heart, I would have waited forever . . . but you made it very clear that would never happen. So I traveled to the four corners of the world and acquired those wives, but all I wanted was you. I would have been true to you.'

'You say that now, after keeping the secret about Allegra hidden from me for decades? Our whole life would have been based on a lie. You are naïve, indeed, about women if you think that would ever have been a happy union.'

Placing my hands against my cheeks, I murmured a single word of dissent. As a soldier, he thought only of two sides to every encounter: forward or retreat. But I had preferred to leave that battlefield many years ago because I had grown tired of fighting for my place in the Pisan circle of brilliance. Instead, I found my own way, far from the places where I had been wounded so badly by the men who deserted me. Byron left. Shelley died. Mary deserted me. And Trelawny was part of it. It was so much easier to hold him at a distance after I had moved away.

Perhaps that had been a mistake, but at least it had been mine to make.

'Claire, if you could ever absolve me of my sins—'

The door opened and Paula strolled in, chatting amicably with Raphael. Georgiana dashed around them and came at me, wrapping her arms around my legs in a tight hug. As the mood shifted, Trelawny moved to the window and said no more.

Paula must have sensed something because her glance fastened on me, then moved to Trelawny and back again. 'Did we interrupt something?'

'Not at all.' I smiled down at my great-niece and stroked her hair. 'We were about to discuss the meeting with Teresa Guiccioli. Did you hear from her, Trelawny?'

'She sent a note with her servant an hour ago,' he answered, his tone flat and distant, as if he spoke from far away. 'Apparently, her health is quite fragile, so she cannot travel far from the Villa Gamba outside Ravenna. But she would be quite agreeable to having us to tea there tomorrow afternoon—'

'Splendid.' Paula clapped her hands. 'How long will it take us to make the trip?'

'Perhaps an hour.' Trelawny shrugged. 'She still lives in her family home near the woods of Filetto.'

A little shiver passed through me. We would travel on the very road where an assassin had tried to shoot Byron.

'Did she sound eager to make our acquaintance? Or simply polite?' Paula slid on to the settee and poured herself a cup of tea, adding only a little milk and sugar.

He strolled back toward our little group and reached into his jacket pocket, presenting a letter. 'You may judge for yourself, if you like.'

'Perhaps not . . .' I began. Never having received any communication from Teresa, I had some hesitation about hearing her words spoken aloud. It made her too real. Too immediate. Especially since I had to mentally prepare myself to be in the presence of the woman who took my place in Byron's life.

'*Si*, you must read it.' Raphael took his place beside Paula. Quickly, Georgiana hopped on to his lap.

Trelawny held out the letter. 'Perhaps Claire could read it
to us since it is written in Italian, and my translation skills
pale in comparison to hers.'

'Of course.' Unfolding the letter, I scanned the shaky handwriting that stretched across the page – smallish letters that
seemed to fade in and out of circles and loops.

I cleared my throat and began to read . . .

Dear Signora Clairmont,

I was most surprised to learn that you are in Ravenna,
though I had heard that you still lived in Italy. As I am
somewhat of an invalid at this point, I rarely leave my
family's home but would be delighted to receive you and
your family for tea, if you are willing to make the journey.

Would four o'clock tomorrow be suitable? If so, please
send word with Trelawny and I shall send my carriage
for you. It should be a fine day for travel.

I look forward to making your acquaintance after all
these long years that have passed. We have much to
discuss.

Teresa G.

I lowered the letter.

'She sounds very amicable,' Paula said with a note of
surprise. 'A gracious offering, to be sure.'

Raphael nodded. 'The Gamba family is well known in
Emilia-Romagna for their generosity – and their courage during
the Risorgimento.'

'Indeed,' Trelawny echoed. 'But it is your decision, Claire.
Do you want to see her?'

I could not respond.

Feeling the thin parchment letter between my fingers, I
resisted the impulse to tear it into a hundred shreds. Even
though she had been like a second mother to Allegra, I had
never wanted to meet this woman. Ever. It felt like finding a
lost object that had been discarded into the dust heap with
careless scorn – I had not wanted to see or hear about her
again after Byron died. It was easier to pretend that she
had not existed at all, or to think of her as a viper who had

slithered into my Eden with a destructive allure. But now, reading her letter, her words showed the kindness that Shelley had described to me.

Perhaps kinder than I would have been to her if the situation had been reversed.

'I think we must accept,' I said with finality. 'After reading her warm invitation, it would seem rude not to journey on a little farther, especially after we have traveled such a distance . . . After I write a note to her, will you send it for me, Trelawny?'

'Yes.' Nothing else.

I could still feel his ire stretching between us. So much was left unspoken, but that would have to wait to be resolved.

Maybe it would never happen.

Some things could not be settled amicably – only forgiven. But I was not ready to confront that possibility yet.

After I wrote a few lines in Italian to Teresa and handed it to Trelawny, I spent a few minutes reading Byron's *confessione*, then a knock was heard at the door. Trelawny swung it open and stepped back to reveal an unexpected visitor.

Lieutenant Baldini.

For an instant, I thought I was hallucinating. The past and present were shifting back and forth so rapidly that I did not know if I was in the here and now or the Ravenna of Byron's memoir . . .

*Palazzo Guiccioli, Ravenna, Italy*
*February 10, 1821*

*Pietro killed a man last night.*

*Tita came into my study during the early morning hours today to tell me about the incident, which apparently occurred near the* Basilica di San Vitale – *a knife fight with an Austrian informant. The body was not found until daylight, so Pietro had been long gone. Murder has become so commonplace in Ravenna that no one asks questions anymore. The bodies are simply buried.*

*Nevertheless, I had Tita set a watch on the palazzo again as I remained in my study.*

*I could not manage any writing after that intelligence – only reading. Dante, of course. But not the* Inferno *. . . his sonnets. In the midst of budding war, my mind turned to love.*

> *Beauty and Duty, these my spirit woo,*
> *And urge their suit, doubting if loyal kiss*
> *To both can e'er be given, and faithful prove . . .*

*Beauty and Duty.*

*I pursued both in my life, but somehow the 'faithful' part eluded me.*

*But I have always tried to be honorable . . . in my fashion, I suppose.*

*Not Dante's.*

*Throwing the book aside, I picked up the Carbonari's new orders for my* turba*; they are ready to fight when we are called to open battle. More rifles. More ammunition. More horses. And still we wait.*

*Never a patient man, I knew I could not stand this much longer. I sent Tita to find Pietro for some news of the Austrian army.*

*While I waited for his return, I glanced at Allegra who still slept on a small couch near the fireplace. I kept her close at all times now, since I did not dare leave her alone until I was able to send her to the convent. It was dangerous to keep a child here, but it was even more perilous to try to move her when all the roads out of the city were blocked by Austrian patrols. I had thought to smuggle her out that night at Dante's Tomb, but the full moon had lit up the sky, providing no cover.*

*In truth, I was reluctant to part from her.*

Mia cucciola.

*She was my only family in Italy, my last connection to Claire and that halcyon summer on the shores of Lake Geneva.*

*Strolling over to where Allegra lay, I brushed back her soft curls, so like her mother's darker tresses – Beauty's Daughter. Sweet and willful. She could read now in Italian, and she loved poetry and music. Again, like her mother. I wished that I could convey all of this to Claire, but I dared not answer her letters – they could be opened along the post road by the Austrians.*

*They would then know of my weakness for my daughter, and she would be in even more danger.*

*It was best to say nothing, even though I know it caused great pain for Claire.*

*Perhaps, after all, I had learned something of the 'duty' that Dante spoke of in his sonnet.*

A quick rap on the door, and it opened for Tita to enter with Pietro in his wake.

The younger man looked pale, though his step still seemed quick and eager. He embraced me heartily with a profusion of Italian, describing the rogue who had set upon him last night. I pointed at Allegra's sleeping figure and motioned for him to lower his voice. The three of us moved to the far side of the room and continued in quiet voices.

Pietro explained how his own attempted assassination occurred near the entrance of San Vitale. A man pretended to be drunk and then attacked him with a knife as he staggered by – luckily, Pietro moved to the side quickly, and the man fell on his own blade.

*Not exactly an epic brawl, but fortunate for Pietro.*

'As he lay dying, he confessed there were bounties on all of us,' Pietro added. 'Especially you, my lord. The Austrians believe that, without your support, the revolution will fade, and they want you dead.'

'I have seen the posters,' I said drily, 'though my likeness is far from flattering.'

Pietro touched my arm. 'Do not take it lightly – they are determined to quash the Carbonari.'

'I have no intention of allowing them to kill me,' I pronounced with a firmness that I was far from feeling. 'They have already tried once in the woods of Filetto, but I will not afford them another opportunity to find me alone.'

Tita nodded, his hand on the long knife tucked into his silk belt.

'My main concern is Allegra. I do not like having her at the palazzo with the Austrian army advancing toward the Po River. They have fifty thousand troops and may choose to attack Ravenna.'

'My father said it is more likely they will pass us and advance

*toward the Neapolitans who are making ready for open battle,'*
*Pietro said. 'She may be safer here at the moment.'*

*Glancing at her, she began to stir. 'Papa?'*

'Sono qui.'

*I am here.*

*And so we agreed to wait . . . for the resurrection of Italy*
*and hope for the world.*

# NINE

'One noble stroke with a whole life may glow,
Or deify the canvass till it shine
With beauty so surpassing all below . . .'

*The Prophecy of Dante*, IV, 28–30

*Ravenna, Italy*
*July 1873*

I extended my hand to Lieutenant Baldini, trying to keep myself fixed in the present. No more thoughts of Byron's memoir – for now. 'This is a . . . surprise.'

'I hope a pleasant one, to be sure.' He bent over my hand in a gracious manner. 'I would not like to think my appearance has caused you any distress.'

'Not at all.' I smiled at his young and handsome face – swarthy skin with a touch of weariness around his eyes. 'I am pleased to see you, even if it is somewhat unexpected.' I cast a pointed glance at my companions.

Paula and Raphael hastily agreed.

Trelawny, however, held back with a wary tilt to his head. 'I sent you word when we stopped in Bagni di Lucca only a couple of days ago, so I am curious as to whether something in my note caused you to travel here. Or was there a new development regarding the stolen Cades sketch?'

He seemed to pause a bit too long. 'The latter . . . and a most astonishing one.'

'You have my attention, sir.' Trelawny moved in closer.

'And mine.' I slid on to a delicately carved chair, thinking if the news was not good, I needed to be in a seated position. 'I am most grateful for the messages that you have sent to us on our way here; it was reassuring to know that you have been working diligently to solve the case.'

'*Prego.*' He paused. 'As I told you in Firenze, the more time passes, the less likely it is that the crimes will be solved – especially with art theft. Stolen artwork is generally smuggled out of the country very quickly. To be honest, I had few leads to pursue, aside from questioning the typical thieves who have been known to us from past arrests. I turned up nothing – until the day before yesterday after I sent Signor Trelawny an update. That is when I received intelligence that the Cades sketch had turned up in Ravenna—'

'Who sent you that information?' Trelawny cut in.

Baldini shook his head. 'I cannot reveal the source, but suffice it to say that it is credible. I alerted the local *polizia*, informing them about the stolen sketch and that I was traveling here to help them "re-acquire" it.'

'But why . . . Ravenna?' Paula's face crinkled in puzzlement. 'Of all places?'

'It is near the coast and would be quite easy to ship to another country from here,' Baldini speculated, but I detected some skepticism behind his words. 'Or perhaps . . .'

'Yes?' I prompted, leaning forward.

He fastened his gaze on me – dark and opaque. 'Word may have spread that your party was traveling here . . . and the thief feels he has unfinished business with you.'

Instantly, I drew back. Could it be the shadow rider – and my attacker? 'Is he after my Byron letters?'

'*Essattemente.*'

'Surely not,' Paula interjected. 'That seems to be an unlikely possibility, to say the least – that someone would journey all this distance for a few letters—'

'Matteo was willing to commit murder to obtain Claire's correspondence,' Trelawny pointed out. 'The thief could be one of his minions who knows the value of anything that relates to Byron or Shelley and is willing to go to great lengths to steal it.'

Would this nightmare over my letters never end? Perhaps I should have sold them to Mr Rossetti, after all.

'Lieutenant, are the ladies in any danger?' Raphael spoke

up, sliding a protective arm around Paula. 'Should we take any precautions?'

'That depends on why you are in Ravenna. Signora Clairmont informed me in Firenze that your intended destination was the Convent of Bagnacavallo . . .' His voice trailed off.

'We were at the convent but decided only recently to extend our trip,' I hastened to explain. 'I wanted to see . . . the Byzantine mosaics, since we were only an hour away. I understand that the Basilica di San Vitale has an exquisite representation of the Empress Theodora wearing a headdress of precious jewels.'

'Ah . . . yes, the courtesan who married Emperor Justinian – a beautiful and ruthless woman who climbed to the highest social position,' Baldini mused.

'How colorful.' With a bright smile, I held up the teapot. 'Would you care for some refreshment, Lieutenant?'

'I will have to decline – I have only just arrived in Ravenna and must stop by the police office – but I am more than happy to accompany you to the basilica tomorrow. It has been many years since I have seen the mosaics at San Vitale, and it is but a short walk from here.'

'Perfect. Shall we say ten o'clock?' My smile remained intact. 'Would anyone else like to join us?'

Paula and Raphael declined, followed quickly by Trelawny.

'It seems as if you and I are the only ones interested in the mosaics, Lieutenant.' I resisted glaring at my companions since Baldini was watching my reactions quite closely and carefully. My suspicions over his sudden appearance increased, but I hid them by simply and calmly pouring myself a cup of tea. 'I look forward to our outing.'

'Then I shall take my leave until tomorrow.' He bowed and let himself out.

Once the door closed behind him, I turned on Trelawny. 'The least you could have done was volunteer to accompany us.'

He coughed lightly. 'I think you can handle the good lieutenant. Besides, I will need to make certain that all the arrangements are set for our afternoon excursion.'

'Paula? Raphael? Will you not come along with me?'

'Aunt Claire, I do not think I could have managed it without blurting out that we came to Ravenna to see Teresa Guiccioli,' she protested. 'Why did you not tell him?'

Shrugging, I sipped my oolong tea. 'I do not know, but his abrupt arrival has made me wary that something else is afoot. He knows more than he is saying about the Cades theft, and I was not ready to reveal our true reason for being here.'

'I agree,' Trelawny said. 'It is highly unusual for a police lieutenant to travel this far based solely on rumors of a stolen piece of artwork, yet he is not a man to be trifled with under any circumstances.'

Georgiana began to squirm around restlessly, demanding tea and biscuits. While Paula and Raphael attended to her, I whispered to Trelawny, 'Baldini's reason for showing up in Ravenna seems a bit contrived – and he would have had two hard days of travel to cover the distance between here and Florence. Could *he* have been trailing us the entire time? Do you trust him?'

'Partly, though I do not believe he read the note that I sent to him. He seemed surprised when I mentioned it. If he is telling the truth about the Cades sketch and his journey here, we have one more ally in Ravenna. If not, we have a formidable enemy. Everything that has happened to us since we left Florence can be explained away, like a ghost in the night – the unseen rider, a mysterious stranger near Vergato, your attacker near Byron's palazzo. It has all been carefully orchestrated to be inconclusive every step of the way, but it feels as if events are converging . . .'

I swallowed hard. 'Say nothing to Paula and Raphael. I shall meet with Baldini tomorrow and see if I can persuade him to reveal anything else to me.'

'And I will be nearby at all times, just in case.'

I sat back, letting these recent developments sink in. I hardly knew what to believe at this point, except that our situation had just worsened. Whether it was Baldini or a stranger behind this plot, we were under greater threat than ever from someone willing to take great risks to achieve his ends.

Even murder?

                              *    *    *

After a dreamless night, I rose early and was ready in the lobby downstairs in my favorite yellow cotton day dress when Baldini appeared.

'You seem refreshed, Signora.' He offered me his arm; careful not to jar my sore shoulder, I slipped my hand through it, allowing him to escort me into the street. Clear, blue skies greeted us – slightly cooler, with a fresh breeze coming in from the east. I did not see Trelawny, but sensed he was close.

'I appreciate that you are willing to make time in your busy schedule to sightsee with someone who could be your mother,' I commented as we strolled past several open-air markets featuring the lush fruit of the region – fresh peaches, apples, and plums. Slowing down to take in their bursts of color in neat little rows, I savored the vast array of produce. 'You must have more important things to do . . . in your investigation.'

He matched his pace to mine. 'I have alerted the local *polizia*, so if the Cades drawing surfaces, I will know immediately. As for the rest, my own mother died years ago, so I am happy to enjoy the company of a woman who is of the same generation. I miss her dearly.'

'One never really recovers from the loss of a mother.'

'Or a child?'

'No, indeed not.' I picked up a random peach and inhaled its soft scent, then casually asked, 'Do you really believe that a thief followed us to Ravenna?'

'*Sì.*'

'And you felt so strongly about it that you traveled night and day to warn us?'

He shrugged. 'That is my job.'

*Perhaps.*

As I started to hand the fruit vendor a few coins for the peach, Baldini brushed my hand away and paid the young woman himself.

'*Grazie*, Lieutenant.' We moved on and I slipped the peach into my small bag, knowing Georgiana would love something sweet later. Baldini seemed so sincere, so honest . . . causing a twinge of guilt over my hidden reason for meeting him and our secret trip to meet Teresa that afternoon. 'On the subject of thieves, may I ask you a question: how well did you know Matteo?'

'Not very. He was an aristocrat from a very old Florentine family, and my late mother was a seamstress in his household.'

*Interessante.* 'And your father?'

His face shuttered down. 'I never knew him.'

'Then we have something in common – I never knew mine either. Even when my mother was dying, she refused to tell me his identity. All I know is that he gave her this piece of jewelry, which she passed on to me.' I touched the gold locket at my throat. 'I rarely take it off since it makes me feel close to the unknown man who fathered me, even though I know nothing about him.'

He studied me silently for a few seconds. 'At least you have some type of memento.'

'It is very precious.' We turned a corner on to the Via Vitale, and I continued, 'If your mother worked for Matteo, you must have known him when you were growing up. Did he ever show you that evil side?'

'No, he was quite kind.' Baldini's voice sounded sad, almost regretful. 'Of course, I was rarely allowed to visit the upper floors since we were considered lower class.'

'I see.' As we slowly passed the genteel palazzos that lined the street, my mind was racing ahead as I tried to piece together the relationship between Matteo and Baldini. 'You must have found it quite painful to arrest him . . . and even more devastating to learn that he had killed himself.'

'He *chose* to become a criminal,' he said without emotion. 'I have seen many men descend into such depths, and I have little sympathy for them. Matteo gambled away his fortune and then survived by lying and stealing – and even killing. If his murder of Father Gianni did not earn him eternal damnation, his suicide certainly will.'

In spite of the sun-flooded brightness of the streets, I shivered. 'Do you think one of his associates stole the sketch? Is that the person we need to fear?'

'Most likely. Matteo led a ring of corruption, and one of the remaining culprits must know the value of your letters from the English poets, but do not worry – I have no doubt that he will reveal himself before long.' Baldini pointed to the austere façade of the basilica that lay ahead. San Vitale. It looked like a fortress with its rough exterior and small, arched windows. 'Shall we go inside?'

I held back. 'Lieutenant, do you think it is a sin to lie?'

'It depends on the reason, I suppose,' he responded quietly. 'Is there something that you want to tell me, Signora?'

My heart beat a little faster – a quick staccato of indecision. 'Only that many men have not always been truthful with me over the years . . . I hope you are not one of them.'

'I am an honest man.'

Searching his face, I thought I saw a flicker of dissembling. 'Then I think we understand each other quite well.'

We moved inside the magnificent basilica with its soaring dome of Baroque frescos and dazzling mosaics. The panels on either side of the apse depicted Theodora and her husband, Emperor Justinian, who was adorned with a halo around his head. It all came to life with jewel-toned colors – almost breathlessly vivid, though we were the only visitors there to appreciate it.

'*Bellissimo*,' my companion exclaimed.

Tilting my head back, I could make out the triumphal arch's depiction of a purple-robed Christ-figure flanked by the apostles – all bathed in gold. He was handing a martyr's crown to Saint Vitale.

'Saints and sinners . . . Only art this beautiful could make the combination so attractive.' Baldini's mouth quirked upwards in an ironic expression. 'Ever it was thus, I suppose.'

'As a converted Catholic, I would have to agree with you.' I laughed softly. 'Perhaps the artist's role is to bear witness to his own truth: that art transcends such matters.'

We strolled around the main section silently, taking in the two chapels and the mullioned windows – and even more stunning mosaics of flowers, angels, and even peacocks. Amidst such beauty, I could almost forget the reason I had come to Ravenna.

*Almost.*

Eventually we circled back to the entrance and took one

last look at the soul-stirring artistry, and I thought I spied Trelawny just outside the door.

'Our last meeting in *Firenze* was in a church – and now we are here,' I finally spoke up as I lit a candle for Allegra. 'Somehow it seems fitting, though I cannot say why.'

'Signora Clairmont, you never answered my question.' He repeated it, this time in Italian.

'I thought I did.'

He paused for a few moments, then shrugged and escorted me out. After I assured him that Trelawny would fetch me, he kissed my hand and bid me farewell. As I watched him walk away, I detected an air of wariness before he crossed the street, his glance darting back and forth, as if watching for someone lurking in the shadows. Baldini seemed nervous.

After the lieutenant was no longer visible, Trelawny appeared at my side. 'Did you learn anything new?'

'Not really.'

'Then we must follow our plan while we wait for the shadow rider's next move – I will arrange for Teresa's carriage to await us.' Without another word, he ushered me back to the Al Cappello.

Hours later, on the way to meet la Guiccioli in her luxurious carriage, I recounted an abbreviated version of my encounter with Baldini to Paula, while Trelawny sat silently next to her. Raphael sat outside with the driver – and Georgiana, giving her a chance to play at handling the horses.

'I was poised to tell Baldini about our excursion this afternoon, but I held back.' Watching the scenery change from the flat, bare landscape to thickets of tall pines as we approached the woods of Filetto, I struggled to explain to Paula without revealing more about the shadow rider. 'When Baldini said his mother often did seamstress work for Matteo – and they benefited from his generosity – I felt uneasy. Do you think it is possible that he is more deeply involved with the theft than he has led us to believe?'

'It does seem odd that he came to Ravenna on a rumor about the Cades sketch.' Paula leaned back against the green silk cushions next to me. 'What do you think, Mr Trelawny?'

He sat across from us, distant and aloof again, in his formal jacket and trousers. In spite of his dutiful protectiveness, he had not forgotten our argument yesterday.

*Oh, my friend, I wish I could take the words back . . .*

One corner of his mouth twisted upward. 'The lack of money can make men do evil – as did Matteo. If Baldini spent his youth poor and fatherless, he may have been quite attached to the one man who showed kindness to his mother and him. Then again, in our brief acquaintance with Baldini, I cannot see him as a totally corrupt officer. Perhaps he was simply trying to protect Matteo after his arrest . . . I cannot say for certain. But this day is about Allegra, as well – not only the stolen drawing.'

'I somehow feel they are connected,' I added.

'We shall know soon enough.' He sounded almost uninterested, but I knew it masked his deep anger. There was so much left unresolved between us that it might be better to not even try to repair our friendship.

'So we may tie up both matters.' Paula cleared her throat, obviously sensing the tension between us. 'If Lieutenant Baldini locates the sketch and Signora Guiccioli has the missing pieces about Allegra, our quest may come to an end today – one way or another. What will you do then, Mr Trelawny?'

He averted his head to watch the passing forest. 'I shall return to England, of course. My life is there.'

*And mine is here.*

'I see.' Paula nudged me slightly as if to prompt me to ask him to stay in Italy a little longer, but I kept my lips sealed shut.

We rolled on with only the sound of carriage wheels in the gravel from that point until we reached the Villa Gamba – the three-storied Baroque structure that I remembered Byron mentioning in his memoir. A pleasant country home of red brick and green shuttered windows. But within its walls, Byron and Teresa's family had plotted revolution. In honor of this place, I brought along Shelley's and his letters in my bag and had pocketed the final page of Byron's *confessione* to read at the villa . . . it seemed fitting to conclude my reading of the memoir here.

The carriage halted, and a footman instantly appeared to usher us inside. The interior was just as quietly elegant, with marble floors, elaborately carved furniture, and gilt-framed paintings. It bespoke old wealth – the many generations who lived and died here, all linked through family ties. So different from my own life untethered to a permanent home.

We entered the parlor to find Teresa lounging in a sunlit parlor with flowered wallpaper and overstuffed chairs. A fire had been lit – even on such a warm day. A lady's room.

The tea service had already been set out with an elaborately painted pot and china cups.

'*Buongiorno.*' She held out her hand to Trelawny.

'It is good to see you again after so many years,' Trelawny said, then he did the introductions as we each seated ourselves. As I settled into a needlepoint chair closest to her, I found myself somewhat surprised at her tiny, delicate form. Almost ethereal, with white hair and soft, unlined cheeks of rose and pearl. Her smile, open and friendly.

I wanted to hate her but could not do so.

'You are most kind to receive us at such short notice,' I began in Italian, 'and to send your carriage.'

'It is my pleasure,' she responded in her native tongue. 'My days are quite solitary now, so having visitors is a welcome treat, especially ones who remind me of my youth.'

Now it was my turn to smile. 'And yet we never met.'

'Such a shame.'

Teresa asked Paula to serve tea while she exchanged polite conversation with the rest of us. Trelawny stood off to the side, struggling to follow with his shaky command of the language. Teresa seemed particularly taken with Georgiana and asked many questions about her age and interests, as she played with her doll on a window seat. 'You had no children of your own?' I asked, handing her a teacup.

'Sadly – no.' She sipped the tea. 'And this house was built for the sound of little ones' laughter. When I was a girl, I spent all of my summers here with my brother, Pietro, roaming the woods and picking flowers along the river. *Paradiso.* It seems a bit lonely now that I am the only one left.'

Ah, yes . . . we shared the bond of outliving many of those whom we loved most in the world.

'Speaking of children, that is the reason we have come to

Ravenna.' I waved off Paula's offer of tea, not sure that I could manage it with my inner tumult of emotions. I gave a quick summary of events during the last fortnight, including Trelawny's revelation about Allegra.

She blinked in surprise. 'But this is unbelievable . . . She died during the typhus epidemic at the convent.'

'Are you certain?' Trelawny pressed.

'*Si.*' Teresa's hand began to shake and she set the cup in its saucer. 'It was April of 1822 – a chaotic time. The revolution had collapsed . . . and we were all under threat of arrest as the Austrians sought out those who had conspired against them. My brother, Pietro, fled to Pisa, and my father and I soon followed, but Byron stayed on because Allegrina had developed a fever. He wanted to remain close to Bagnacavallo in case she worsened—'

'Which she did,' I said with a sharp edge to my voice.

'The nuns told him she was out of danger on the fifteenth of April – I recall the date because Byron sent me a letter on that day, saying he was much relieved to hear the news—' She broke off. 'Then I learned five days later that the Abbess contacted him to say Allegra had succumbed to her illness. I had no communication from Byron for weeks. When I did hear from him, he did not mention her demise. Nor did he speak of it to me afterwards.'

Raphael's brows knit in confusion. 'But he told Trelawny a very different story when they were in Greece.'

'Byron said he faked his daughter's death because she was still in danger, even though the possibility of open war had passed.' Trelawny moved his shoulders in a perplexed shrug. 'Perhaps he felt his role with the Carbonari would cause the Austrians to take revenge – someone had tried to assassinate him only months before, and an intruder had broken into Allegra's room at the convent—'

'*Dio mio,*' Teresa gasped. 'I did not know.'

'I still cannot believe that someone would harm an innocent child,' Paula murmured, her eyes shifting to Georgiana as if to reassure herself that she was still there.

'Nor I.' Trelawny's face turned grim. 'It shook Byron to the core.'

Teresa leaned forward and touched my arm for an instant. 'I only wish I knew more. All I can say is that I loved Allegra as if she were my own daughter, and I would have done anything to protect her from harm.'

A twinge of pain tugged at my heart. Certainly, I did not doubt her sincerity, but it brought back my hurt feelings of knowing my daughter called another woman *Mama*. Trying to maintain my fragile control, I shifted my regard away from Teresa to the bric-a-brac around the parlor, with its lovely oriental figurines and delicate painted vases – until I spied a small, oval-shaped curio with Byron's image. The familiar, handsome face that haunted me.

Teresa rose to her feet. 'May I show you the garden? It is in full bloom.'

'*Si.*' I stood as well.

Had she seen my reaction?

As she gestured toward the open French doors, I insisted that everyone else finish their tea. Paula nodded, and I suspected she understood only too well that I needed time for a private conversation with Teresa.

We emerged into a small, carefully manicured garden with a variety of rose bushes – all shapes and colors, each one as fragrant as the sweetest perfume. Matching my steps to Teresa's slower ones, we moved along a path of tiny stones toward an arbor made of lattice work and covered with vines.

'I am sorry, Signora Clairmont, if I caused you any upset.' Teresa plucked a large, pink rose. 'I thought I had put away any . . . mementos from Byron.'

She *had* seen my discomfort.

'There is no need to apologize,' I assured her. 'Seeing his face simply caught me off guard – I keep no such portraits, nor did I receive one from him.'

Inhaling the rose as we ambled along, she added, 'I have very few mementos either.'

I sighed, knowing that meant she had many, many keepsakes. 'You are a gracious, thoughtful hostess, Signora Guiccioli, especially under these circumstances, knowing we both had liaisons with the same man. I loved him first and had his child, and you loved him last . . .'

'And had no child.' Regret threaded through her voice. 'It seems strange that we are bonded through Byron, especially when neither of us could really possess him. He was too brilliant, too restless to ever commit to one woman, and now he belongs to the ages . . . the hero who died for Greek independence.'

'So true. He is worshipped there as his idol George Washington is in America.' Our shoes crunched the stones underfoot. 'At least he died fighting for freedom.'

She paused. 'Do you miss him?'

'Every day – and you?'

'Every hour.'

'But you married again, did you not?' I queried as we reached the arbor.

'Ah, yes – it was a late-life marriage to Marquis de Boissy.' She gave a short laugh. 'All I can say is that I was lonely, and he offered devotion. A good man.'

'But not *him*.'

'No.'

We said no more about Byron. There was nothing left to say. We had been drawn into his world of passion and love – a heady orbit that took us beyond where ordinary mortals lived. But after his star died out, we came crashing back to earth, left dreaming of those distant skies.

'I can only hope that Allegra *did* survive the typhus,' she said. 'Even the possibility must give you some comfort.' She handed me the rose. 'I must return to my guests, but please stay here until you are ready to join us.'

'*Grazie*, Signora.' Watching her as she moved back toward the palazzo, my lifetime of resentment seemed to dissolve. She was a warm and gentle woman who happened to love the man who broke my heart. If only we had met before this, I might not have wasted so much energy blaming *her* for my grief and loss. She could not help but love him.

Byron broke all the rules of society, as did we all. Trelawny, Shelley, Mary, Teresa, me. We paid the consequences.

And still, were I to live it all over again, I would do the same.

Except giving up Allegra.

Leaning my head against the arbor, I tucked the rose into my hair, then reached into my pocket to retrieve Byron's last memoir page that I had tucked in there before we left for Ravenna. Slowly, I unfolded it, ready to read his final entry . . .

*Palazzo Guiccioli, Ravenna*
*February 20, 1821*

*The entire country is in turmoil. Word reached us that the Neapolitans have made ready for war as the Austrians advance south. Then the rest of Italia shall follow. A free Italy. Any day now, I will lead my turba into battle.*

*As if to signal the great change coming, another strong thunderstorm has blown in from the east, lighting the sky and shaking the very foundations of the house. It reminded me of the thunderous squalls in Geneva during summer of 1816, except that I can hear the Adriatic Sea roaring off to the east of Ravenna.*

*I am alone now, except for Tita and the servants.*

*Teresa is still at her father's country villa, and Pietro remains hidden at a remote house deep in the Filetto forest.*

*Allegra is gone.*

*After the Austrians skirted Ravenna, I was able to send her to the convent at Bagnacavallo where she will be safe. The Abbess assured me that she would protect her with her own life, and I receive daily reports, but I miss her intensely. Her little face looking up at me as I read her poetry – so dear and trusting . . .*

*But this is no place for a child. The entire palazzo is an arsenal, full of weapons and Carbonari fighters who come and go at odd hours.*

*I was eating dinner in my study, listening to the wind blowing outside, when Pietro appeared under the cover of night. He said two more Austrians had been killed near Dante's Tomb and the Pope responded by making a declaration against the patriots. It will inflame the situation even more, so we celebrated by drinking Imola wine until the early hours of the morning when he left for his father's house.*

*Waiting for the dawn from my bedchamber, I saw the skies clear and knew it heralded a new day for Italy – and me. We would drive the Austrians out of the country, and I would live out the remainder of my days as a retired military hero, writing poetry and watching Allegra grow into a young woman.*

*Sweet days lay ahead.*

*Then I heard a knock at the door – Tita.*

*After I bade him enter, he strode in and conveyed the most astonishing news: the Neapolitans have backed down and have vowed not to engage the Austrians in open battle, leaving us in the north without military support. Some of the Carbonari have been betrayed and are fleeing the country. So much for unity and revolution.*

*In that moment, I realized it was over.*

*The dream of a free* Italia.

*Stunned, I sank on to the bed, asking Tita to repeat the message* verbatim. *Instead, he handed me the note.*

*'It is settled, then?' I said after scanning it twice.*

*'Si . . . the Austrians will now have their revenge on the Neapolitans once they take control again, and we must prepare ourselves for whatever retribution they intend to rain down on Ravenna. We are between the two fires, cut off from the north and unable to receive aid from the south, and shall burn if we are not careful.'*

*'The Carbonari will need to disband, and we shall have to move out of the province,' I thought aloud, calculating how best to protect my household. 'The Shelleys are in Pisa . . . we shall join them, and I can bring Allegra—'*

*'Perhaps that is not a good idea.'*

*I turned very still. Something in his tone told me she was not out of danger yet.*

*'A man broke into her room at the convent intending to do her harm. The Abbess arrived in time to save her life and was able to describe the intruder – it sounded like di Breme's servant—'*

*'Damn it all to hell and back.' I crumbled the message and threw it aside. 'By God, I will find him . . . make him pay for this.'*

*Tita nodded his massive head. 'My spies are already making inquiries.'*

*Rising from my dejected perch, I felt resolve flood through me. The revolution might be over, but the fight to keep Allegra safe would go on. Forever.*

*Back in Geneva, before she was born, I suspected her life would be a perilous journey, and it was confirmed. Not only because of my involvement with the Carbonari . . .*

*Moving to my writing desk, I motioned Tita over. 'Come, we must plan.'*

That was Bryon's last entry.

As I came back to the present in Teresa's rose-filled garden, I recalled his words that Allegra's life would be a 'perilous journey.' Why? What had happened during di Breme's visit in the summer of 1816 that would cause his servant, Stefano, to attack me and then later stalk both Byron and Allegra in Italy?

Byron knew but did not dare to tell anyone – not even Trelawny.

But perhaps Teresa knew something more than she realized; it was worth mentioning to her. After that . . . perhaps my quest would be finished.

Removing the rose from my hair, I tucked it and the memoir page back in my pocket and took one last glance around the garden before I made my way back to the villa. Such peace and beauty. But it was time to leave. As I strolled along the flower-lined path, I had to acknowledge that Trelawny had brought me a gift when he gave me Byron's memoir – an opportunity to reconsider the past and learn a few more truths about events that had appeared to be cruel at the time. I would always be grateful to Trelawny for this charity.

I would forgive him, fully and completely – and perhaps he could forgive me for leaving him after that night in Pisa.

Quickening my pace, I entered the French door with a smile that quickly faded as I beheld the scene inside.

A visitor had arrived while I lingered in the garden: Lieutenant Baldini.

He waved me forward. 'Please, Signora Clairmont, you must join us.'

Paula and Raphael huddled on the settee, clutching each

other's arms. Teresa stood behind them, but Trelawny and Georgiana were nowhere to be seen.

*Put on a brave front.*

'It seems you have followed us here for some reason, Lieutenant,' I said in a calm voice as I stepped inside. 'We were simply on a pleasant outing to see an old friend.'

His expression was a mask of stone. 'Please close the door behind you – we have an important matter to settle, and I would like to keep it private.'

A warning voice whispered in my mind as I followed his direction.

Moving toward the chair near the fireplace, I commented, 'I thought you told me at San Vitale you were an honest man.'

'He is.' Matteo stepped from behind him, holding a knife to the lieutenant's neck. 'But I am not.'

*Matteo* – the man who had killed Father Gianni and tried to kill me in the Boboli Gardens in Firenze. The devil. Evil incarnate.

My body stiffened in shock. 'But you are dead. You committed suicide on the journey to the Rome prison.'

'Not likely.' He smiled. 'Do you think my network is limited only to Firenze? It is far larger than you can imagine – with members who were more than happy to assist me in faking my own death. One of the prison coach drivers slipped me a potion on the road that simulated death. When my "body" arrived in Rome, I was immediately taken to the undertaker where my body was exchanged with a dead man's and buried quickly. Then I was revived in due course by the doctor who created the potion. An excellent plan, do you not think?'

Raphael spat at him.

'*You* are the shadow rider,' I said. Paula was crying, but I dared not take my eyes off Matteo. The wild look in his eyes told me he was capable of anything right now, including murder. 'I understand why you would fake your own death, but why follow us?'

'For the English poets' letters, of course. They were *mine* that night at the Boboli Gardens,' he grated out. 'I was desperate for money then – and I still am now. You were right, Signora. I did have your apartment vandalized – but you had the letters locked away and my men had no time to break into your desk, so they took only the Cades drawing. A valuable item, though unknown to me the time, and I compliment them on their ingenuity. But I wanted the letters, too. My informants told me you were heading to Ravenna – quite convenient since my buyer lives there as well. So, I sent word of the sketch on to him, then I trailed you, knowing you would bring along the letters; it proved surprisingly easy and enjoyable to toy with you at every step of the way. I followed you to the *terme*, then Vergato where I ran into the child whom I chose not to harm – *then*. When I saw you, Signora, on Via Cavour yesterday, I struck you as a final insult. And now the journey is over – and I want those letters. My buyer will pay a huge sum for both.'

'You monster,' Paula choked out between sobs.

'I do not have them with me.' Technically true – since my bag had slipped behind the chair cushion.

'You lie.' He pressed the knife further into Baldini's neck, causing a bright red spot of blood to appear. Gauging whether the men could overpower Matteo, I spied a pistol tucked into the waist of his pants. They might manage to take the knife from him but could end up shot in the process.

Raphael jumped up, but Matteo yelled at him to sit. Paula seized her lover's hand and pulled him down next to her again. 'Aunt Claire, give Matteo the letters. *Please*.'

I knew she was thinking about Georgiana and what might happen when she returned with Trelawny; it was unlikely that Matteo would just take the letters and quietly depart. He could not leave any witnesses.

Matteo narrowed his eyes – slits of vicious intent. 'I know you have the letters since I already searched your room at the Al Cappello and found only this.' He held up the rest of Byron's memoir. 'Oh, and I also took back the ivory bookmark left there – you will have no need of it.'

Cold fury rose up inside me at the thought of him rummaging through my things – yet again. 'Your father did not give it to you, did he?'

'You are learning about my true nature – no, I stole it.' One side of his mouth twisted upwards in a mockery of a smile.

'Now bring the letters to me, Signora Clairmont, or I will kill this man.'

Baldini tried to jerk away, but Matteo tightened his grasp with the strength of a desperately insane man.

'Do not harm him,' I finally said, reaching behind the chair cushion to retrieve my bag. I held it out. 'They are in here.'

'Walk it over to me,' he instructed.

Teresa tried to stop me, but I shook my head. 'My family means more to me than these pieces of paper.' As I approached him, I saw Byron's memoir peeping out of his jacket pocket. *Bastardo.*

'Give the bag to Baldini.' Matteo inched them toward the fireplace, still keeping the blade firmly in place.

After I did so, Matteo threw Byron's memoir on to the fire, and I gasped. 'No!'

The pages curled into bright yellow and red fire, then crinkled into nothingness. I felt a tear stream down my cheek. 'Why did you destroy it?'

'It was meant to be consumed in fire like the other copy,' he murmured, 'so there will be no record left.'

But how did he know the other copy had been burned?

'And none of you will be left either.' His voice turned low and deep like a rumbling volcano, ready to erupt and envelop us all. 'I shall burn this villa down, too.'

He was insane.

I prayed that Trelawny would not return with Georgiana – she had to survive.

All rational thought evaporated as Matteo moved the knife across Baldini's throat – he meant to kill him, then probably shoot the rest of us. Paula and I cried out for mercy at the moment Trelawny appeared in the doorway. He slammed his walking stick against Matteo's head. Matteo tried to block its blunt force with his arm, releasing Baldini who fell to the floor with his neck bleeding profusely.

Matteo flicked his knife and sliced across Trelawny's shoulder. He staggered slightly but managed to strike Matteo across the face with the back of his hand. Roaring with fury in response, Matteo lunged at Trelawny and they tumbled on to the floor as Raphael moved into the fray. He kicked Matteo's chest, causing him to wince in pain.

Then Trelawny fell backwards, breathing heavily, to reveal Matteo with the knife in his chest – almost exactly like the stabbing he had inflicted on Father Gianni. As I watched the growing scarlet stain on his jacket, Paula and Teresa attended to Baldini's wound.

I rushed over to Trelawny and helped him up, careful not to touch his shoulder. 'Are you all right?'

He nodded.

'Georgiana?'

'I hid her in the kitchen when I heard Matteo's voice – she is fine.'

At that point, I slipped my arms around Trelawny. 'My dear friend . . . you risked your life for me,' I whispered in a shaky voice. 'For all of us.'

'For love.'

We stood like that for a few moments, then I heard Paula say, 'The memoir is burned . . . gone.'

Leaning back in Trelawny's embrace, I looked over at the fireplace and saw only ashes.

'But we saved the letters,' Baldini said in a hoarse tone as he propped himself up on one elbow.

Matteo groaned weakly. 'Signora Clairmont.'

I heard the death rattle in his throat and, in spite of everything that he had done, I let Trelawny go and knelt down next to the dying man. 'Pray for God's leniency, Matteo.'

He gave a laugh that turned into a cough. 'I deserve damnation . . . but I will not be alone.'

'If you atone for your lies and crimes, you may yet find grace.' I made the sign of the cross over his face, but he seized my hand.

'I did not lie about Father Gianni – all I desired was the money, but he wanted everything connected to your daughter destroyed. You never knew his surname . . . it was Costa. Gianni Costa.' Matteo's released my hand as his head dropped to one side and his last breath exhaled in one long, deep sigh.

I stared down at his lifeless form in shock. *Costa*. The last name of di Breme's servant. Was Father Gianni somehow related to him? Feeling thwarted once again by Matteo, I wanted to shake the truth out of his still, dead body. But now that he was dead, would I ever know?

*Al diavolo!*

He had defeated us.

*Convent of San Giovanni, Bagnacavallo, Italy*
*March 1821*

*Allegra's story*

I felt cold.

As I sat in the convent courtyard, it seemed so barren with its empty spaces and skeletal trees reaching into gray skies.

Weeks have passed and still my papa has not visited me. The nuns were kind – especially the Abbess – but they rarely spoke to me aside from school lessons; they moved silently from room to room, heads bowed, their black dresses trailing like silent waves. The other girls whispered about me, so I avoided them. I was left on my own much of the time and yet I was never allowed to leave the convent's high, stone walls – ever since the man broke into the convent.

Now the nuns watched me all the time.

I missed my papa.

When I lived with him in Ravenna, he loved to hear me sing, calling me *bella Allegrina*, from the Italian word *allegro*. Fast and cheerful. He said I was a child of music and light.

My life was so happy until he sent me here.

It felt like a prison after living with my papa in his palazzo.

Sighing, I pulled my heavy woolen shawl tighter against the winter wind that blew in from the coast, causing me to cough . . .

I waited for Sister Anna to call me to tea, which she served every afternoon, promising that Papa would come to see me the next day.

But tomorrow never seemed to come.

So I would retreat to my room with its narrow bed and thick white walls and write to Papa, hoping my loving words would melt his heart and he would want to see me. I etched my initials in the window so he would not forget me.

Night after night, I would dream that he arrived as the spring flowers began to bloom.

My papa.

Would he ever come?

# TEN

'The age which I anticipate, no less
Shall be the Age of Beauty . . .'

*The Prophecy of Dante*, IV, 71–72

*Villa Gamba, near Ravenna*
*1873*

Trelawny and I stood in front of Teresa's fireplace looking down into the ashes of what had been Byron's memoir. It had burned very quickly, leaving only dusty echoes of what had been. All the passion and dreams for a united Italy ended in flames – along with his memories of the Carbonari.

'I am sorry I could not save even a page.' He sifted through what was left with the poker but came up with nothing.

'But I have the last one in my pocket – I put it there earlier to read alone.' Covering his hand with mine, I stopped his efforts. 'The important thing is everyone is safe, and we shall never have to confront Matteo ever again. He is truly dead.'

'He is indeed.' Lieutenant Baldini walked with halting steps into the parlor; a bandage had been placed around the cut on his neck. 'I just had two local police officers remove Matteo's body to Ravenna. We shall then have it taken back to Firenze and buried quietly without telling his elderly aunt – the only Ricci family member who is still alive.'

'Will you tell her what actually happened – choose honesty – unlike Aunt Claire who seems to have withheld information from us?' Paula asked as she joined us, accompanied by Raphael; he carried Georgiana as if she were the most precious cargo – and she was, indeed.

I offered her a look of apology.

'It is kinder to lie sometimes.' Baldini shook his head. 'She has suffered enough because of his disgrace when he was arrested . . . I will simply have him placed in the family tomb; she will never know. The man whose body already lies there shall remain.'

Raphael set Georgiana down, and she immediately ran over to me. I held her close.

'Do not fear; I will find who is responsible for helping Matteo with his evil plot – and his buyer in Ravenna.' Baldini's voice hardened. 'And I must apologize to all of you about Trelawny's note. When he sent word that you had taken a detour to Bagni di Lucca, I never received the message because I had already left Firenze – my investigation led me to one of Matteo's money lenders who believed that Matteo might have been behind the vandalism at your apartment, though I did not know he was still alive. When I heard a rumor that the Cades drawing might surface in Ravenna, I headed here to catch the thief *and* warn you.'

'Do you have the sketch?' I inquired, ready to pardon his actions.

'It is safely locked away in the Ravenna police station – the officers found it in Matteo's hotel room.'

A sense of elation rose up inside of me. I had regained my drawing of the obelisk in Boboli Gardens – the place that had been the scene of one of my greatest sorrows and greatest joys. And now it would provide me with the means to support my family . . . no more poverty.

I leaned down briefly and placed a soft kiss on Georgiana's head. My dear one would want for nothing.

As I straightened, I saw Paula and Raphael share a smile of deep love.

Ah . . . the world seemed to have righted itself finally.

'What about the quest for your daughter, Signora?' Baldini queried. 'Will you continue your search?'

My eyes slid to Trelawny. 'I . . . I am not sure. We have reached a blind alley, with no other place to go. There are no records at the convent that would indicate Allegra survived, and Signora Guiccioli is the only one still alive who would remember anything that could help us.' I took in a deep breath. 'It may be enough to know that she *may* have lived.'

Baldini bowed. 'Then I shall see you in Firenze.'

Trelawny escorted him out as Teresa rejoined us.

I took her hands in mine and switched to Italian. 'I regret that this day brought so much upset into your home, but I am happy to have finally met you.'

'And I, you.' She clasped my fingers tightly, her eyes bright with affection. 'It should have happened long ago. I can only say again that I wish I knew more about your daughter. Allegra was happy in Ravenna – I know that – though she missed her true *mamina*.' She produced a small stack of letters tied with a blue ribbon. 'I have a present for you. These are my brother Pietro's letters of Byron's final days.'

'But I cannot take them—'

'I insist.' Teresa placed them in my palm. 'It is my way of sharing Byron with you. We both meant something to him in the end . . .'

Words failed me, but I managed to give her a quick embrace of true gratitude for a woman who had lost almost as much as I had. 'I have one last thing to ask you: did Byron ever mention Ludovico di Breme?'

'The poet?' Her brows knit in puzzlement. 'Only in passing – they knew each other in Ravenna and both loved Dante.'

'Nothing else? Especially about his servant, Stefano?'

'Not that I remember – I am sorry.' She gave a helpless shrug. 'Will you return immediately to Firenze?'

'In a day or two,' I replied.

'Please come back for tea before you go,' she said. 'I never finished showing you the rose garden.'

'It will be my pleasure.' I placed Pietro's letters in my bag with Byron's – they belonged together as two soldiers who fought side by side in Greece. 'Then we will travel home, with perhaps a short stop at the Convent of Bagnacavallo along the way.'

'I understand . . . Please convey my regards to the Abbess; it has been a long time since I have seen her – it is unfortunate that she could not remember anything about Allegra's time at the convent.'

'She was sort of . . . helpful,' Paula added diplomatically.

Sighing, I swung my gaze to the small portrait of Byron;

it seemed to fit the spot perfectly now. 'She researched the convent's records, but they stated only that Allegra died of the typhus—'

'Why would she need to look at any records?' Teresa's brows rose. 'The Reverend Mother was a novice then – in charge of Allegra – so she was there at the time. I thought she must have told you.'

'But Byron's memoir said Sister Anna took care of my daughter,' I said, a spark of confusion igniting within me.

'The Abbess *is* Sister Anna.'

The room turned utterly silent. Everything in place. But somehow also changed with the echo of her words.

When Trelawny returned, I moved toward him slowly and deliberately. 'We must return to Bagnacavallo tomorrow,' I pronounced. We had traveled too far on this journey not to pursue this one last detour. 'Apparently, the Abbess withheld an important fact from us: *she* was the novice in charge of Allegra.'

Trelawny grew very still. 'So she knows the truth?'

'Yes.' And I would move heaven and earth to find it.

*Il cielo et la terra.*

Heaven and earth.